Ruth Fielding at Snow Camp

Alice B. Emerson

DODO PRESS

RUTH FIELDING

AT SNOW CAMP

OR

LOST IN THE BACKWOODS

BY

ALICE B. EMERSON

CONTENTS

Ruth Fielding at Snow Camp

CHAPTER I

A LIVELY TIME

"I don't think we'd better go home that way, Helen."

"Why not? Mr. Bassett won't care—and it's the nearest way to the road."

"But he's got a sign up—and his cattle run in this pasture," said Ruth Fielding, who, with her chum, Helen Cameron, and Helen's twin brother, Tom, had been skating on the Lumano River, where the ice was smooth below the mouth of the creek which emptied into the larger stream near the Red Mill.

"Aw, come on, Ruthie!" cried Tom, stamping his feet to restore circulation.

The ground was hard and the ice was thick on the river; but the early snows that had fallen were gone. It was the day after Christmas, and Helen and Ruth had been at home from school at Briarwood Hall less than a week. Tom, too, who attended the Military Academy at Seven Oaks, was home for the winter holidays. It was snapping cold weather, but the sun had been bright this day and for three hours or more the friends had enjoyed themselves on the ice.

"Surely Hiram Bassett hasn't turned his cows out in this weather," laughed Helen.

"But maybe he has turned out his bull," said Ruth. "You know how ugly that creature is. And there's the sign."

"I declare! you do beat Peter!" ejaculated Tom, shrugging his shoulders. "We are only going to cut across Bassett's field—it won't take ten minutes. And it will save us half an hour in getting to the mill. We can't go along shore, for the ice is open there at the creek."

"All right," agreed Ruth Fielding, doubtfully. She was younger than the twins and did not mean to be a wet blanket on their fun at any time; but admiring Helen so much, she often gave up her own inclinations, or was won by the elder girl from a course which she thought wise. There had been times during their first term at Briarwood Hall, now just completed, when Ruth had been obliged to take a different course from her chum. This occasion, however, seemed of little moment. Hiram Bassett owned a huge red herd-leader that was the terror of the countryside; but it was a fact, as Helen said, that the cattle were not likely to be roaming the pasture at this time of year.

"Come on! " said Tom, again. "The car was to go down to the Cheslow station for father and stop at the mill for us on its return. We don't want to keep him waiting. "

"And we've got so much to do to-night, Ruthie! " cried Helen. "Have you got your things packed? "

"Aunt Alvirah said she would look my clothes over, " said Ruth, in reply. "I don't really see as I've much to take, Helen. We only want warm things up there in the woods. "

"And plenty of 'em, " advised Tom. "Bring your skates. We may get a chance to use them if the snow isn't too heavy. But up there in the backwoods the snow hasn't melted, you can bet, since the first fall in November. "

"We'll have just the loveliest time! " went on Helen, with her usual enthusiasm. "Tom and I spent a week-end at Snow Camp when Mr. Parrish owned it, and when we knew he was going to sell, we just *begged* papa to buy it. You never saw such a lovely old log cabin—"

"I never saw a log cabin at all, " responded Ruth, laughing.

They had climbed the steep bank now and started across the pasture in what Tom called "a catter-cornering" direction, meaning to come out upon the main road to Osago Lake within sight of the Red Mill, which was the property of Mr. Jabez Potter, Ruth's uncle.

Ruth Fielding, after her parents died, had come from Darrowtown to live with her mother's uncle at the Red Mill, as was told in the first volume of this series, entitled "Ruth Fielding of the Red Mill; Or, Jasper Parloe's Secret. " The girl had found Uncle Jabez very hard to get along with at first, for he was a good deal of a miser, and his finer feelings seemed to have been neglected during a long life of hoarding and selfishness.

But through a happy turn of circumstances Ruth was enabled to get at the heart of her crotchety uncle, and when Ruth's very dear friend, Helen Cameron, planned to go away to school, Uncle Jabez was won over to the idea of sending Ruth with her. The girls were now home for the winter holidays after spending their first term at Briarwood Hall, where they had made many friends as well as learning a good many practical and necessary things. The fun and work of this first term is all related in "Ruth Fielding at Briarwood Hall; Or, Solving the Campus Mystery, " which is the second volume of the Ruth Fielding Series.

And now another frolic was in immediate prospect. Mr. Cameron, who was a very wealthy dry-goods merchant, had purchased a winter camp deep in the wilderness, up toward the Canadian line, and Christmas itself now being over, Helen and Tom had obtained his permission to take a party of their friends with them to the lodge in the backwoods —Snow Camp.

It was really Helen's party. Besides Ruth, she had invited Madge Steele, Jennie Stone, Belle Tingley, and Lluella Fairfax to be of the party. She had invited one other girl from Briarwood, too; but Mary Cox had refused the invitation. "The Fox, " as her school-fellows called her, had been under a cloud at the end of the term, and perhaps she might have felt somewhat abashed had she joined the party of her school-fellows at Snow Camp.

Tom had invited his chum at school, who was Madge Steele's brother Bob, and another boy named Isadore Phelps. With Mr. Cameron himself and Mrs. Murchiston, the lady who had been the twins' governess when they were small, and several servants, the party were to take train at Cheslow the next day for the northern wilderness.

The trio of friends, as they hurried across Hiram Bassett's pasture, were full of happy anticipations regarding the proposed trip, and they chatted merrily as they went on. Halfway across the field they passed along the edge of a bush-bordered hollow. Their skating caps— Tom's white, Ruth's blue, and Helen's of a brilliant scarlet— bobbed up and down beside the hedge, and anybody upon the other side, in the hollow, might have been greatly puzzled to identify the bits of color.

"For mercy's sake! what's that? " ejaculated Helen, suddenly.

The others fell silent. A sudden stamping upon the frozen ground arose from beyond the bushes. Then came a reverberating bellow.

Tom leaped through the bushes and looked down the hill. There sounded the thundering of pounding hoofs, and the boy sprang back to the side of his sister and her chum with a cry.

"Run! " he gasped. "The bull is there—I declare it is! He's coming right up the hill and will head us off. We've got to go back. He must have seen us through the bushes. "

"Oh, dear me! dear me! " cried his sister. "What will we do—"

"Run, I tell you! " repeated Tom, seizing her hand.

Ruth had already taken her other hand. With their skates rattling over their shoulders, the trio started back across the field. The bull parted the bushes and came thundering out upon the plain. He swerved to follow them instantly. There could be no doubt that he had seen them, and the bellow he repeated showed that he was very much enraged and considered the three friends his particular enemies.

Ruth glanced back over her shoulder and saw that the angry beast was gaining on them fast. It was indeed surprising how fast the bull could gallop—and he was very terrible indeed to look upon.

"He will catch us! he will catch us! " moaned Helen.

"You girls run ahead, " gasped Tom, letting go of his sister's hand. "Maybe I can turn him—-"

"He'll kill you! " cried Helen.

"Come this way! " commanded Ruth, suddenly turning to the left, toward the bank of the open creek. The current of this stream was so swift that it had not yet frozen—saving along the edges. The bank was very steep. A few trees of good size grew along its edge.

"We can't cross the creek, Ruthie! " shrieked Helen. "He will get us, sure. "

"But we can get below the bank—out of sight! " panted her chum. "Come, Tom! that beast will kill you if you delay. "

"It's our caps he sees, " declared Master Tom. "That old red cap of Nell's is what is exciting him so. "

In a flash Ruth Fielding snatched the red cap from her chum's head and ran on with it toward the bank of the creek. The others followed her while the big bull, swerving in his course, came bellowing on behind.

CHAPTER II

A SURPRISING APPEARANCE

Helen was sobbing and crying as she ran. Tom kept a few feet behind the girls, although what he could have done to defend them, had the big bull overtaken him, it would be hard to say. And for several moments it looked very much as though Hiram Bassett's herd-leader was going to reach his prey.

The thunder of his hoofs was in their ears. They did not speak again as they came to the steep bank down to the open creek. There, just before them, was an old hollow stump, perhaps ten feet high, with the opening on the creek side. All three of them knew it well.

As Helen went over the bank and disappeared on one side of the stump, Tom darted around the other side. Ruth, with the red cap in her hand, stumbled over a root and fell to her knees. She was right beside the hollow stump, and Helen's cap caught in a twig and was snatched from her hand.

As Ruth scrambled aside and then fairly rolled over the edge of the bank out of sight, the cap was left dangling right in front of the stump. The bull charged it. That flashing bit of color was what had attracted the brute from the start.

As the three friends dived over the bank—and their haste and heedlessness carried them pell-mell to the bottom—there sounded a yell behind them that certainly was not emitted by the bull. Goodness knows, he roared loudly enough! But this was no voice of a bull that so startled the two girls and Tom Cameron—it was far too shrill.

"There's somebody in that tree! " yelled Tom.

And then the forefront of the bull collided with the rotten old stump. Taurus smashed against it with the force of a pile-driver— three-quarters of a ton of solid flesh and bone, going at the speed of a fast train, carries some weight. It seemed as though a live tree could scarcely have stood upright against that charge, let alone this rotten stump.

Crash!

The rotten roots gave way. They were torn out of the frozen ground, the stump toppled over, and, carrying a great ball of earth with it, plunged down the bank of the creek.

Tom had clutched the girls by their hands again and the three were running along the narrow shore under shelter of the bank. The bull no longer saw them. Indeed, the shock had thrown him to the ground, and when he scrambled up, he ran off, bellowing and tossing his head, in an entirely different direction.

But the uprooted stump went splash! into the icy waters of the creek, and as it plunged beneath the surface—all but its roots—the trio of frightened friends heard that eyrie cry again.

"It's from the hollow trunk! I tell you, some body's in there! " declared Tom.

But the uprooted stump had fallen into the water with the opening down. If there really was anybody in it, the way in which the stump had fallen served to hold such person prisoner.

Ruth Fielding was as quick as Tom to turn back to the spot where the old stump had been submerged; but Helen had fallen in her tracks, and sat there, hugging her knees and rocking her body to and fro, as she cried:

"He'll be drowned! Don't you see, he *is* drowned? And suppose that bull comes back? "

"That bull won't get us down here, Nell, " returned her brother, laying hold of the roots of the hollow tree and trying to turn it over.

But although he and Ruth both exerted themselves to the utmost, they could barely stir the stump. Suddenly they heard a struggle going on inside the hollow shell; as well, a thumping on the thin partition of wood and a muffled sound of shouting.

"He's alive—the water hasn't filled the hollow, " cried Ruth. "Oh, Tom! we must do something. "

"And I'd like to know what? " demanded that youth, in great perturbation.

The stump rested on the shore, but was half submerged in the water for most of its length. The unfortunate person imprisoned in the hollow part of the tree-trunk must be partly submerged in the water, too. Had the farther end of the stump not rested on a rock, it would have plunged to the bottom of the creek and the victim of the accident must certainly have been drowned.

"Why don't he crawl out? Why don't he crawl out? " cried Ruth, anxiously.

"How's he going to do it? " sputtered Tom.

"Can't he dive down into the water through the hole in the tree and so come up outside? " demanded the girl from the Red Mill, irritably. "I never saw such a fellow! "

Whether this referred to Tom, or to the unknown, the former did not know. But he recognized immediately the good sense in Ruth's suggestion. Tom leaped out upon the log and stamped upon it. Helen screamed:

"You'll go into the creek, too, Tom! "

"No, I won't, " he replied.

"Then you'll make the stump fall in entirely and the man will be drowned. "

"No, I won't do that, either, " muttered Master Tom.

He stamped upon the wooden shell again. A faint halloo answered him, and the knocking on the inner side of the hollow tree was repeated.

"Come out! Come out! " shouted Tom, "Dive down through the water and get out. You'll be suffocated there. "

But at first the prisoner seemed not to understand—or else was afraid to make the attempt.

"Oh, if I only had an axe! " groaned Master Tom.

"If you cut into that tree you might do some damage, " said his sister, now so much interested in the prisoner that she got up and came near.

Ruth saw Helen's red cap high up on the bank and she scrambled up and got it, stuffing it under her coat again.

"We'll keep *that* out of sight, " she said.

"If it hadn't been for that old red thing, " growled Tom, "the bull wouldn't have chased us in the first place. "

But all of them were thinking mainly of the person in the hollow of the old stump. How could they get this person out?

And the answer to that question was not so easily found—as Tom had observed. They could not roll the stump over; they had no means of cutting through to the prisoner. But, suddenly, that individual settled the question without their help. There was a struggle under the log, a splashing of the water, and then a figure bobbed up out of the shallows.

Ruth screamed and seized it before it fell back again. It was a boy— a thin, miserable-looking, dripping youth, no older than Tom, and with wild, burning eyes looking out of his wet and pallid face. Had it not been for Ruth and Tom he must have fallen back into the stream again, he was so weak.

They dragged him ashore, and he fell down, shaking and chattering, on the edge of the creek. He was none too warmly dressed at the best; the water now fast congealed upon his clothing. His garments would soon be as stiff as boards.

"We've got to get him to the Mill, girls, " declared Tom. "Come! get up! " he cried to the stranger. "You must get warmed and have dry clothing. "

"And something hot to drink, " said Ruth. "Aunt Alviry will make him something that will take the cold out of his bones. "

The strange boy stared at them, unable, it seemed, to speak a word. They dragged him upright and pushed him on between them. The bull had run towards the river and had not come back; so the friends, with their strange find, hurried on to the public road and crossed the bridge at the creek, turning off into the orchard path that led up to the Red Mill.

"What's your name? " demanded Tom of the strange boy.

But all the latter could do was to chatter and shake his head. The icy water had bitten into his very bones. They fairly dragged him between them for the last few yards, and burst into Aunt Alvirah's kitchen in a manner "fit to throw one into a conniption! " as that good lady declared.

"Oh, my back, and oh, my bones! " she groaned, getting up quickly from her rocking chair by the window, where she had been knitting. "For the good land of mercy! what is this? "

All three of the friends began to tell her together. But the little old woman with the bent back and rheumatic limbs understood one thing, if she made nothing else out of the general gabble. The strange boy had been in the water, and his need was urgent.

"Bring him right in here, Tommy, " she commanded, hobbling into Mr. Potter's bedroom, which was the nearest to the kitchen, and thereby the warmest. "I don't know what Jabez will say, but that child's got to git a-twixt blankets right away. It's a mercy if he ain't got his death. "

They drew off the stranger's outer clothing, and then Aunt Alviry left Tom to help him further disrobe and roll up in the blankets on Mr. Potter's bed. Meantime the old woman filled a stone water-bottle with boiling water, to put at his feet, and made a great bowl of "composition" for him to drink down as soon as it was cool enough for him to swallow.

Ruth wrung out the boy's wet garments and hung them to dry around the stove, where they began immediately to steam. As she had noticed before, the stranger's clothing was well worn. He had no overcoat— only a thick jacket. All his clothing was of the cheapest quality.

Suddenly Helen exclaimed: "What's that you've dropped out of his vest, Ruthie? A wallet? "

It was an old leather note-case. There appeared to be little in it when Ruth picked it up, for it was very flat. Certainly there was no money in it. Nor did there seem to be anything in it that would identify its owner. However, as Ruth carried it to the window she found a newspaper clipping tucked into one compartment, and, as it was damp, too, she took this out, unfolded it, and laid it carefully on the window sill to dry. But when she looked further, she saw inside the main compartment of the wallet a name and address stenciled, It was:

JONAS HATFIELD

SCARBORO, N. Y.

"Sec, Helen, " she said to her chum. "Maybe this is his name—Jonas Hatfield. "

"And Scarboro, New York! " gasped Helen, suddenly. "Why, Ruthie! "

"What's the matter? " returned Ruth, in surprise.

"What a coincidence! "

"What is a coincidence? " demanded Ruth, still greatly amazed by her chum's excitement.

"Why this boy—if this is his wallet and that is his name and address—comes from right about where we are going to-morrow. Scarboro is the nearest railroad station to Snow Camp. What do you think of that? "

Before Ruth could reply, the sound of an automobile horn was heard outside, and both girls ran to the door. The Cameron automobile was just coming down the hill from the direction of Cheslow, and in a minute it stopped before the door of the Potter farmhouse.

CHAPTER III

THE NEWSPAPER CLIPPING

The Red Mill was a grist mill, and Mr. Jabez Potter made wheat-flour, buckwheat, cornmeal, or ground any grist that was brought to him. Standing on a commanding knoll beside the Lumano River, it was very picturesquely situated, and the rambling old farmhouse connected with it was a very homey-looking place indeed.

The automobile had stopped at the roadside before the kitchen door, and Mr. Cameron alighted and started immediately up the straight path to the porch. He was a round, jolly, red-faced man, who was forever thinking of some surprise with which to please his boy and girl, and seldom refused any request they might make of him. This plan of taking a party of young folk into the backwoods for a couple of weeks was entirely to amuse Tom and Helen. Personally, the dry-goods merchant did not much care for such an outing.

He came stamping up the steps and burst into the kitchen in a jolly way, and Helen ran to him with a kiss.

"Hullo I what's all this? " he demanded, his black eyes taking in the grove of airing garments around the stove. "Tom been in the river? No! Those aren't Tom's duds, I'll be switched if they are! "

"No, no, " cried Helen. "It's another boy. "

And here Tom himself appeared from the bedroom.

"I thought Tom could keep out of the river when the ice was four inches thick—eh, son? " laughed Mr. Cameron.

His children began to tell him, both together, of the adventure with the bull and the mysterious appearance of the strange boy.

"Aye, aye! " he said. "And Ruth Fielding was in it, of course—and did her part in extricating you all from the mess, too, I'll be bound! Whatever would we do without Ruth? " and he smiled and shook hands with the miller's niece.

"I guess we were all equally scared. But it certainly was my fault that the old bull bunted the hollow stump into the creek. So this boy can thank me for getting him such a ducking, " laughed Ruth.

"And who is he? Where does he come from? "

Ruth showed Mr. Cameron the stencil on the inside of the wallet.

"Isn't that funny, Father? " cried Helen. "Right where we are going— Scarboro. "

"If the wallet is his, " muttered Mr. Cameron.

"What do you mean, sir? " questioned Ruth, quickly. "Do you think he is a bad boy—that he has taken the wallet——"

"Now, now! " exclaimed Mr. Cameron, smiling at her again. "Don't jump at conclusions, Mistress Ruth Fielding. I have no suspicion regarding the lad——How is the patient, Aunt Alviry? " he added, quickly, as the little old woman came hobbling out of the bedroom where the strange boy lay.

"Oh, my back, and oh, my bones! " said Aunt Alviry, under her breath. But she welcomed Mr. Cameron warmly enough, too. "He's getting on fine, " she declared. "He'll be all right soon. I reckon he won't suffer none in the end for his wetting. I'm a-goin' to cook him a mess of gruel, for I believe he's hungry. "

"Who is he, Aunt Alviry? " asked the gentleman. Aunt Alvirah Boggs was "everybody's Aunt Alviry, " although she really had no living kin, and Mr. Jabez Potter had brought her from the almshouse ten years or more before to act as his housekeeper.

"Dunno, " said Aunt Alvirah, shaking her head in answer to Mr. Cameron's question. "Ain't the first idee. You kin go in and talk to him, sir. "

With the wallet in his hand and the three young folk at his heels, both their interest and their curiosity aroused, Mr. Cameron went into the passage and so came to the open door of the bedroom. Mr. Potter slept in a big, four-post bedstead, which was heaped high at this time of year with an enormous feather bed. Rolled like a mummy in the blankets, and laid on this bed, the feathers had plumped up about the vagabond boy and almost buried him. But his eyes were wide open—pale blue eyes, with light lashes and eyebrows, which gave his thin, white countenance a particularly blank expression.

"Heigho, my lad! " exclaimed Mr. Cameron, in his jolly way. "So your name is Jonas Hatfield, of Scarboro; is it? "

"No; sir; that was my father's name, sir, " returned the boy in bed, weakly. "My name is Fred. "

And then a brilliant flush suddenly colored his pale face. He half started up in bed, and the pale blue eyes flashed with an entirely different expression. He demanded, in a hoarse, unnatural voice:

"How'd' you find me out? "

Mr. Cameron shook his head knowingly, and laughed.

"That was a bit of information you were keeping to yourself—eh? Well, why did you carry your father's old wallet about with you, if you did not wish to be identified? Come, son! what harm is there in our knowing who you are? "

Fred Hatfield sank back in the feathers and weakly rolled his head from side to side. The blood receded from his cheeks, leaving him quite as pale as before. He whispered:

"I ran away. "

"Yes. That's what I supposed, " said Mr. Cameron, easily. "What for? "

"I—I can't tell you. "

"What did you do? "

"I didn't say I did anything. I just got sick of it up there, and came away, " the boy said, sullenly.

"Your father is dead? " asked the gentleman, shrewdly.

"Yes, sir. "

"Got a mother? "

"Yes, sir. "

"Doesn't she need you? "

"No, sir. "

"Why not? "

"She's got Ez, and Peter, and 'Lias to work the farm. They're all older'n me. Then there's the two gals and Bob, who are younger. She don't need me, " declared Fred Hatfield, doggedly.

"I don't believe a mother ever had so many children that she didn't sorely miss the one who was absent, " declared Mr. Cameron, quietly. "Tell me how you came away down here, "

Brokenly the boy told his story—not an uncommon one. He had traveled most of the distance afoot, working here and there for farmers and storekeepers. He admitted that he had been some weeks on the road. His being in that hollow stump in Hiram Bassett's field was quite by accident. He was passing through the field, making for the main road, when he had seen Ruth, Helen, and Tom, and stepped behind the tree so as not to be observed.

"What made you so afraid of being seen by anyone? " demanded Mr. Cameron, at this point. "Do you think your folks are trying to find you? "

"I—I don't know, " stammered the lad.

This was about all his questioner was able to get out of him.

"You'll be cared for here to-night—I'll speak to Mr. Potter, " said Mr. Cameron. "And in the morning I'll decide what's to be done with you. "

"Why, Dad! we're going——"

Tom had begun this speech when his father warned him with a look to be still.

"You'll be all right here, " pursued Mr. Cameron, cheerfully. "Aunt Alviry and Ruth will look after you. Why! I wouldn't want better nurses if *I* was sick. "

"But I'm not sick, " said Fred Hatfield, as the little old woman hobbled in with a steaming bowl. His eyes were wolfish when he saw the gruel, however.

"No, you're not so sick but that a good, square meal would be your best medicine, I'll be bound, " cried the gentleman, laughing.

He went out to the mill then and was gone some moments; when he returned he called Helen and Tom to come with him quickly to the car.

"Remember and be ready as early as nine o'clock, Ruth! " called Helen, looking back as she climbed into the automobile.

When her friends had bowled away up the frozen road, Ruth came back into the kitchen. Aunt Alvirah was still in the bedroom with their strange guest. Of a sudden the girl's eye caught sight of the newspaper clipping laid on the window sill to dry.

Mr. Cameron had placed the old wallet belonging to Fred Hatfield's father on the table when he came out of the bedroom. Now Ruth picked it up, found it dry, and went to the window to replace the clipping in it. It was the most natural thing in the world for Ruth to glance at the slip of paper when she picked it up. There is nothing secret about a newspaper clipping; it was no infringement of good manners to read the article.

And read it Ruth did when she had once seen the heading—she read it all through with breathless attention. Her rosy face paled as she came to the conclusion, and she glanced suddenly toward the bedroom as she heard Aunt Alvirah's voice again.

Dropping the old wallet on the table, Ruth folded the clipping and hastily thrust it into the bosom of her frock. She did not dare face the old woman when she appeared, but kept her back turned until she was sure the color had returned to her cheeks. And all the time she helped Aunt Alvirah get supper, Ruth was very, very silent.

CHAPTER IV

THE MYSTERIOUS BEHAVIOR OF FRED HATFIELD

Uncle Jabez Potter came in from the mill after a time. He was a gaunt, gray-faced man, who seldom smiled, and whose stern, rugged countenance had at first almost frightened Ruth whenever she looked at it. But she had fortunately gotten under the crust of Mr. Potter's manner and learned that there was something better there than the harsh surface the miller turned to all the world.

Uncle Jabez hoarded money for the pleasure of hoarding it; but he had been generous to Ruth, having put her at one of the best boarding schools in the State. He could be charitable at times, too; Aunt Alvirah could testify to that fact. So could a certain little lame friend of Ruth Fielding, Mercy Curtis, who was attending Briarwood Hall as the result of the combined charity of Uncle Jabez and Dr. Davison, of Cheslow.

But it is said that "charity begins at home"; when charity begins in a man's very bed, that seems a little too near! At least, so Mr. Potter thought.

"What's this I hear about a vagabond boy in my bed, Aunt Alviry? " he demanded, when he came in.

"The poor child! " said the old woman. "Oh, my back, and oh, my bones! Come in and see him, Jabez, " she urged, hobbling toward the passage.

"No. Who is he? What is he here for? That Cameron talks so fast I never can get the rights of what he's saying till afterward. Says the boy belongs up there where he wants to take Ruth to-morrow? "

"He has run away from his home at Scarboro, Uncle, " said Ruth.

"Young villain! A widder's son, too! " said her uncle.

"He says his father is dead, " said Ruth, hesitating.

"I venture to say! " exclaimed Jabez Potter. "And he's in my bed; is he? "

He came back to this as being a reason for objection.

"Now, now, Jabez, " said Aunt Alvirah, soothingly. "He ain't hurted the bed. He was wet—the coat frozen right on him—when they brought him in. I had to git him atween blankets jest as quick as I could. And your bedroom isn't so cold as the rooms upstairs. "

"Well? " grunted Mr. Potter.

"Before bedtime I'll make him up a couch in here near the fire and put your bed straight for you. "

"Young vagabond! " grunted Mr. Potter. "Don't know who he is. May rob us before morning. Perhaps he come here for just that purpose. "

"That's not possible, Uncle, " said Ruth, laughing. She told him the story of their adventure with the bull and Fred Hatfield's appearance. Yet all the time she looked worried herself. There was something troubling the girl of the Red Mill.

Ruth took the tray into the bedroom with the supper that Aunt Alvirah had prepared. There was a flaming red spot in the center of each of the boy's pallid cheeks, and his eyes were still bright. He had no little fever after the chill of his plunge into the creek. But the fever might have been as much from a mental as a physical cause.

It was on Ruth's lips to ask the boy certain questions. That newspaper clipping fairly burned in the bosom of her frock. But his suppressed excitement warned her to be silent.

He was hungry still. It was plain that he had been without proper food for some time. But in the midst of his appreciation of the meal he asked Ruth, suddenly:

"Wasn't there anything in that wallet when you gave it to that man, Miss? "

"No, " she replied, truthfully enough.

"No. He didn't say there was, " muttered the boy, and said not another word.

Ruth watched him eat. He did not raise his light eyes to her. The color faded out of his cheeks. She knew that it was actual starvation that kept him eating; but he was greatly troubled in his mind. She went back to her own supper, and remained very quiet all through the evening.

Later Aunt Alvirah made up the couch with plenty of blankets and thick, downy "comforters, " and when Ruth had gone to bed the boy came out into the kitchen and left Uncle Jabez free to seek his own repose. But though the whole house slept, Ruth could not—at first. Long after it was still, and she knew Aunt Alvirah was asleep and Uncle Jabez was snoring, Ruth arose, slipped on a warm wrapper and her slippers, and squeezing something tightly between her fingers, crept down the stairs to the kitchen door. She unlatched it softly and let it swing open a couple of inches.

There was a stir within. She waited, holding her breath. She heard the couch creak. Then came the sound of a shuffling step.

The moonlight lay in a broad band under the front window. Into this radiance moved the figure of the vagabond boy, shrouded in a blanket. He came to the table and he felt around until he found the wallet. He had doubtless marked it lying there by the window before Aunt Alvirah had put the lamp out and left him.

He seized the wallet and opened it wide. He shook it over the table. Then Ruth heard him groan:

"It's gone! it's gone! "

He stood there, shaking, and dropped the leather case unnoticed. For half a minute he stood there, uncertain and—Ruth thought—sobbing softly. Then the boy approached the garments hung upon the chairs about the stove, wherein the coal fire was banked for the night.

He stopped before he touched his underclothing. All these garments were well dried by this time; but Aunt Alvirah had wished them left there to be warm when he put them on in the morning. Ruth knew exactly what Fred Hatfield had in his mind. The vagabond boy was determined to dress quietly and secretly leave the miller's house.

But when Master Fred touched the first garment Ruth rattled the door latch ever so lightly. Fred stopped and turned fearfully in that direction. His lips parted. She could see that he was panting with fear.

Ruth rattled the latch again. He ran back to his couch and plunged into the comforters with a gasp. Ruth pulled the door quietly to and stood there, shivering in the dark, wondering what to do. She knew that the boy had it in his mind to escape. She did not wish to arouse Uncle Jabez. Nor did she wish the strange boy to depart so secretly.

Mr. Cameron expected to find him here when he came in the morning, she was sure. Although Mr. Cameron only supposed him an ordinary runaway, and perhaps wished to advise him to return to his mother, Ruth knew well that Fred Hatfield's was no ordinary case of vagabondage.

Ruth hesitated on the stairs for some minutes. Uncle Jabez snored. There was no further movement from the boy on the couch.

She was growing very cold. Ruth could not remain there on the stairs to guard the boy all night. Something desperate had to be done—and something very desperate she did!

She unlatched the door again as quietly as possible. She pushed it open far enough to slip through into the kitchen. There was no movement from the boy—not a sound. Nor did Ruth dare even look in his direction.

She crept across the kitchen floor to the stove. She reached the garments hung upon the chair backs. She selected one and withdrew in a hurry to the staircase, and so ran up to her room.

"There! " she thought, shutting her door and breathing heavily. "If he wants to run away he can; but he'll have to go without his trousers! "

CHAPTER V

OFF FOR THE BACKWOODS

It was still dark when Ruth awoke and slipped down to the kitchen again. But she heard her uncle rattling the stove grate. He was a very early riser. She peered into the kitchen and saw the grove of drying clothing, so knew that her trick of the night before had kept Fred Hatfield from running away.

Therefore she merely dropped the boy's nether garments inside the kitchen door and scurried back to her own room to dress by candle-light. She heard Aunt Alvirah stumbling about her room and groaning her old, old tune, "Oh, my back, and oh, my bones! " As soon as Ruth was dressed she ran in to see if she could do anything for the old woman.

"Ah, deary! what a precious pretty you be, " said the old woman, hugging her. "I'm so glad to see you again after your being away so long. And your Uncle's that proud of you, too! He often reads the reports the school teacher sends him—I see him doing that in the evening. He keeps the reports in his cash-box, just as though they was as precious as his stocks and bonds. Yes-indeedy! "

"You are so glad to have me at home, Aunt Alvirah, that I feel guilty to be going away again so soon, " Ruth said.

"No, honey. Have your good times while ye may, my pretty creetur. It's mighty nice of the Camerons to take you away with them. You go and have a good time. Your trunk's all packed and ready, and your young friend, Helen, would be dreadful disappointed if you didn't go. Now, let's go down and git breakfast. Jabez has been up for some time and I heard him just go out to the mill. That boy must be up and dressed by now, for if he had been sick, Jabez would have hollered up the stairs about it. "

She was right. Fred Hatfield was completely dressed when they came into the kitchen. Ruth did not look at him, but busied herself with the details of getting breakfast. She did not speak to him, nor did Fred speak to her. But Aunt Alvirah was as cheerful and as chatty as ever.

Uncle Jabez was never talkative; but he was no more taciturn this morning than was their guest. The boy ate his breakfast with downcast eyes and only said timidly, at the end of the meal:

"I'm real obliged for your kindness, Mr. Potter. I think I'm all right again now. Can't I do some work for you to pay—"

"I don't need another hand at the mill—and I couldn't make use of a boy like you at all, " said Mr. Potter, hastily. "You wait till Mr. Cameron comes here this morning. "

Ruth saw that there was an understanding between her uncle and Mr. Cameron regarding this boy. But Fred said, still hesitating:

"If—if I can't do anything to repay you, I'd rather go on. I was making for Cheslow. I'll get a job—"

"You wait here as you're told, boy, " snapped Uncle Jabez, and the runaway shrank into his chair again and said nothing more.

Breakfast at the Red Mill was always early; it had been finished before seven o'clock on this clear winter morning. It was a fine day when the sun appeared, and Ruth's mind—at least, a *part* of it! —delighted in the thought of the journey to be taken into the great woods to the north and east of Osago Lake. She had several little things to do in preparation; therefore she could not be blamed if she lost sight of Fred Hatfield occasionally.

Suddenly, however, she found that he had left the kitchen. She cried up the stairs to Aunt Alvirah:

"Have you seen him, Auntie? Where is he? "

"Where's who? " returned the old woman.

"That boy. He's not here. "

"For the land's sake! " returned Aunt Alvirah. "I dunno. Didn't your uncle tell him to wait for Mr. Cameron here? "

"But he's gone! " exclaimed Ruth; and picking up her cap she pulled it on, and likewise her sweater, and went out of the house with a bang. He was not on the road to Cheslow. She could see that, straight before the mill, for a mile. She ran down to the gate and looked along the river road, up stream. No figure appeared there. Nor in the other direction—although the Camerons' car would appear from that way, and if the runaway went in that direction he would surely run right into the Camerons.

"He slipped out of the back door—towards the river, " she whispered.

Back she ran into the house. She caught up her skates in the back hall and burst out upon the back porch, which was partly enclosed. There was the figure of Fred Hatfield on the ice—some distance, already, from the shore.

Ruth ran eagerly down to the shore. She had no idea what young Hatfield intended; but she was well aware that he could get across the Lumano if he chose; the ice was thick enough.

She quickly clamped the skates upon her shoes, and within five minutes was darting off across the ice.

Hatfield heard the ring of her skates within a very few moments; he threw a glance over his shoulder, saw her, and then began to run. It was a feeble attempt to escape, for unless some accident happened to Ruth, she could easily overtake him.

And she did so, although he ran straight ahead, and ran so hard that finally he slipped and fell, panting, to his knees. Ruth was beside him before he could rise.

"Don't you be such a ridiculous boy! " she commanded, seizing the lad by the shoulder, as he attempted to rise. "You mustn't run away. Mr. Cameron expects to find you at the mill, and you must stay. And they'll be here, ready to take the train from Cheslow, shortly. "

"I—I don't want to stay here, " stammered the boy. "I—I don't want to see that man again. "

"But he expects to see you, and I could not let you go before he comes. "

"You're just the meanest girl I ever saw! " cried Hatfield, almost in tears. "I'd got away in the night if it hadn't been for you. "

Ruth fairly giggled at that—she couldn't help it.

"Well, don't you be nasty about it, " she said. "You are a dreadfully foolish boy—"

"What do you know about me? " he gasped, turning to look at her finally with frightened eyes.

"I know that running away isn't going to help you, " Ruth Fielding said, with returning gravity.

"You think that man—that Cameron man—will take me back? "

"Back where? "

"To—to Scarboro? "

"I don't know. "

"I tell you I won't go, " the boy cried. "I won't go. "

"But we're all going up there this very day, " said Ruth, slowly. " Mr. Cameron, and Helen and Tom, and some other girls and boys. I'm going, too—"

"*Going where*? " shrieked Fred Hatfield, actually shaking with terror, and as pale as a ghost.

"We're off for the backwoods—up Scarboro way. Mr. Cameron is going to take us for a fortnight to Snow Camp. And you—"

With another wild cry Fred Hatfield crumpled down upon the ice and burst into a tempest of sobbing. He beat his ungloved hands upon the ice, and although Ruth could not help feeling contempt for a boy who would so give way to weakness she could not help but pity him, too.

For Ruth Fielding had more than an inkling of the trouble that so weighed Fred Hatfield down, and had made him an outcast from his home and friends.

CHAPTER VI

ON THE TRAIN

When the Cameron automobile arrived at the Red Mill that forenoon Fred Hatfield sat gloomily upon the porch steps. Ruth kept an eye on him from the doorway. Mr. Cameron seemed to understand their position when he came up the walk, and asked Ruth:

"So, he wants to leave; does he? "

Ruth merely nodded; but Fred Hatfield scowled at the dry-goods merchant and turned away his head.

"Now, young man, " said Mr. Cameron, standing in front of the sullen boy, with his legs wide apart and a smile upon his ruddy face, "now, young man, let's get to the bottom of this. You confide in me, and I will not betray your confidence. Why don't you want to live at home? "

"I don't want to—that's all, " muttered Fred Hatfield, shortly. "And I *won't.* "

Mr. Cameron shook his head. "I hate to see one so young so obstinate, " he said. "It may be that your mother and brothers and sisters find you a sore trial; perhaps they are glad you are not at home. But until I am sure of that I consider it my duty to keep an eye on you. I want you to come along with us to-day. "

"I know where you are going. This girl has told me, " said the light-haired youth, nodding at Ruth. "You're going up to Scarboro. "

"Yes. And I propose to take you with us. We'll see whether your mother wants you or not. "

"You don't know what you're doing, sir! " gasped Fred Hatfield, crouching down upon the step.

"I certainly do not know what I am doing, " admitted Mr. Cameron. "But that is your fault, not mine. If you would trust us—"

"I can't! " cried the boy, shaking as though with a chill.

"Then, you come along, young man, " commanded the merchant.

He put a hand upon Fred's shoulder and the boy wriggled out from under it and started to run. But Tom had got out of the automobile and seemed rather expecting this move. He sprang for the other boy and held him.

"Here! hold on! " he cried. "Put on this old overcoat of mine that I've brought along, It's going to be cold riding. Put it on—and then get into the auto with us. Aw, come on! What are you afraid of? We aren't going to eat you. "

Snivelling, but ceasing his struggles, Fred Hatfield got into the coat Tom offered him, and entered the car. Ruth said never a word, but she looked very grave.

Uncle Jabez came to the door of the mill and Ruth ran to him and kissed the old miller goodbye. Not that he returned the kiss; Uncle Jabez looked as though he had never kissed anybody since he was born! But Aunt Alvirah hugged and caressed her "pretty creetur" with a warmth that made up for the miller's coldness.

"Bless ye, deary! " crooned the little old woman, enfolding Ruth in her arms. "Go and have the best of times with your young friends. We'll be thinkin' of ye here—and don't run into peril up there in the woods. Have a care. "

"Oh, we won't get into any trouble, " Ruth declared, happily, with no suspicion of what was before the party in the backwoods. "Goodbye! "

"Good-bye, Ruthie—Oh, my back and oh, my bones! " groaned Aunt Alvirah, as she hobbled into the house again, while Ruth ran down to the car, leaped aboard, and the chauffeur started immediately. Ben, the hired man, had gone on to Cheslow with Ruth's trunk early in the morning, and now the automobile sped quickly over the smooth road to the railroad station.

By several different ways—for Cheslow was a junction of the railroad lines—the young folk who had been invited to Snow Camp had gathered at the station to meet the Camerons and Ruth Fielding. Nobody noticed Fred Hatfield, saving Mr. Cameron and Ruth herself; but the runaway found no opportunity of leaving the party.

Tom had no attention to give the Scarboro boy as he welcomed his own chums.

"Here's old Bobbins and Busy Izzy! " he cried, seeing Bob Steele and his sister, with Isadore Phelps, pacing the long platform as the car halted.

Bob Steele was a big, yellow-haired boy, rosy cheeked and good-natured, but not a little bashful. As Madge, his sister, was a year and a half older than Bob she often treated him like a very small boy indeed.

"Now, Master Cameron! " she cried, when Tom appeared, "don't muss his nice clean clothes. Be careful he doesn't get into anything. Be a good boy, Bobbie, and the choo-choo cars will soon come. "

Isadore Phelps was a sharp-looking boy, with red hair and so many freckles across the bridge of his nose and under his eyes that, at a little distance, he looked as though he wore a brown mask. Isadore seldom spoke without asking a question. He was a walking interrogation point. Perhaps that was one reason why he was known among his mates as "Busy Izzy, " being usually busy about other people's business.

"What do you let her nag you for that way, Bob? " he cried. "I'd shake her, if she was my sister—wouldn't you, Tom? "

"No, " said Tom, boldly, for he considered Madge Steele quite a young lady. "She's too big to shake—isn't she, Bobbins? "

But Bob only smiled in his slow way, and said nothing. The girls were in a group by themselves—Helen and Ruth, Belle and Lluella, Jennie Stone (who rejoiced in the nickname of "Heavy" because of her plumpness) and Madge Steele. Mr. Cameron had gone to the ticket window to make an inquiry. It was Ruth who saw Fred Hatfield making across the tracks to where a freight train was being made up for the south.

"Tom! " she cried to Helen's brother, and he turned and saw her glance.

"By George, fellows! " exclaimed Tom, with some disgust. "There's that chap sneaking off again. We've got to watch him. Come on! "

He ran after the runaway. Busy Izzy was at his ear in a moment:

"What's the matter with him? Who is he? What's he been doing? Is he trying to get aboard that freight? What do you want of him? "

"Oh, hush! hush! " begged Tom. "Your clatter would deafen one. " Then he shouted to Hatfield: "Hold on, there! the train will be in soon. Come back! "

Hatfield stopped and turned back with a scowl. Tom grinned at him cheerfully and added:

"Might as well take it easy. Dad says you're to go along with us, so I advise you to stick close. "

"Pleasant-looking young dog, " said Bob, in an undertone. "What's he done? "

"I don't know that he has done anything, " returned Tom, in the same low tone. "But we're going to take him with us to Scarboro. That is the place he has run away from. "

"Did he run away from home? " demanded Isadore Phelps. "What for? "

"I don't know. But don't you ask him! " commanded Tom. "He wouldn't tell you, anyway; he won't tell father. But don't nag him, Izzy. "

To the great surprise of the young folks, when the train bound north came along, there was a private car attached to it, and in that car the Cameron party were to travel. One of the railroad officials had lent his own coach to the Cheslow merchant, and he and his party had the car to themselves.

There was a porter and a steward aboard—both colored men; and soon after the train started odors from the tiny kitchen assured the girls and boys that they were to have luncheon on the train.

"Isn't it delightful? " sighed Heavy, gustily, in Ruth's ear. "Riding through the country on this fast train and being served with our meals—Oh, dear! why weren't *all* fathers born rich? "

"It's lucky your father isn't any richer than he is, Jennie Stone! " whispered Madge Steele, who heard this. "If he was, you'd do nothing but eat all the livelong day. "

"Well, I might do a deal worse, " returned Heavy. "Father says that himself. He says he wishes my reports were better at Briarwood; but he can't expect me to put on flesh and gain much learning at the same time—not when the days are only twenty-four hours long. "

They all laughed a good deal at Heavy, but she was so good-natured that the girls all liked her, too. What they should do when they reached Snow Camp was the principal topic of conversation. As the train swept northward the snow appeared. It was piled in fence corners and lay deep in the woods. Some ice-bound streams and ponds were thickly mantled in the white covering.

Mr. Cameron read his papers or wrote letters in one compartment; Mrs. Murchiston was the girls' companion most of the time, while Tom and his two chums had a gay time by themselves. They tried to get Fred Hatfield into their company, but the runaway boy would not respond to their overtures.

At the dinner table, when the fun became fast and furious, Fred Hatfield did not even smile. Heavy whispered to Ruth that she never did see a boy before who was so dreadfully solemn. "And he grows solemner and solemner every mile we travel! " added Heavy. "What do you suppose is on his mind? "

Ruth was quite sure she knew what was on the lad's mind; but she did not say. Indeed, all the day long she was troubled by the special knowledge she had gained from the newspaper clipping that she carried hidden in the bottom of her pocket. Should she tell Mr. Cameron about it? Should she speak plainly to Fred himself about it? The nearer they approached Scarboro the more uncertain she became, and the more sullen Fred Hatfield looked.

Ruth watched him a good deal, but so covertly that her girl friends did not notice her abstraction. The short Winter day was beginning to draw in and the red sun was hanging low above the tree-tops when Mr. Cameron announced that the second stop of the train would be their destination. The party—at least, Mr. Cameron, the governess, and the young folk—were to remain at the hotel in

Scarboro over-night. The serving people and the baggage were to go on that evening to Snow Camp.

Fred Hatfield sauntered to the rear of the car and stood looking out of the window in the door. The flagman was on the rear platform, however, and he could not get down without being observed. The stop at this town was brief; then the train sped on through the deep woods.

But suddenly the airbrakes were put on again and they slowed down with a good deal of clatter and bumping.

"We're not at Scarboro yet, surely? " cried Mrs. Murchiston.

"No, no! " Mr. Cameron assured them. "We're stopping from some other cause—why, this is merely a flag station. Not even a station—just a crossing. "

A white-sheeted road crossed the rails. There were two or three houses in sight and a big general store, over the door of which was painted:

EMORYVILLE P. O.

But the train had stopped and the rear brake-man, or flagman, seized his lamp and ran back to wait for the engineer to recall him. It was growing dusk and the lamps had been lighted the length of the train. The general interest of the party drew their attention forward. Ruth, suddenly remembering Fred Hatfield, looked toward the rear of the car. Fred was just going out of the door in the wake of the brakeman.

"Oh, he mustn't go! " whispered Ruth to herself, and leaving her girl companions she ran back to speak to the runaway boy. When she reached the door, Fred had already descended the steps. She saw him run across the tracks, and quick as a flash she sprang down after him.

CHAPTER VII

A RUNAWAY IN GOOD EARNEST

Fred Hatfield, the runaway, was approaching the old, rambling country store at Emoryville Crossroads. It was so cold an evening that there were no loungers upon the high, railless porch which extended clear across the front of the building. Indeed, there was but one wagon standing before the store and probably there were very few customers, or loungers either, inside. The stopping of the train had brought nobody to the door.

As Fred gained the sidewalk in front of the store he glanced back. There was Ruth crossing the tracks behind him.

"You come back! Come back immediately, Fred Hatfield! " she called. "Come back or I shall call Mr. Cameron. "

The girl had been his Nemesis all day. Fred knew he could have given the party the slip at some station, had Ruth not kept such a sharp watch upon him. And here she was on his very heels, when he might have gotten well away.

The next stop would be Scarboro. Fred did not want to appear in Scarboro again. And he had a suspicion that Ruth knew his reasons for desiring to keep away from his home and friends.

He looked wildly about the lonely crossroads. The panting of the locomotive exhaust was not the only sound he heard. The two mules hitched to the timber wagon—the only wagon standing by the store— jingled their harness as they shook their heads. One bit at the other, and his mate squealed and stamped. They were young mules and full of "ginger"; yet their driver had carelessly left them standing unhitched in the road.

Fred gave another glance at Ruth and kept on running. The engineer suddenly whistled for the return of the flagman. But none of the train-hands—nor did the party in the private car—notice the boy and girl who had so incautiously left the train.

"Come back! " commanded Ruth, so much interested in following Fred that she did not notice the lantern of the rear brakeman bobbing along beside the ties. In a moment he swung himself aboard the private car and his lantern described half an arc in the dusk. The engine answered with a loud cough and the heavy train began to move.

But at that moment Fred Hatfield, grown desperate because of Ruth's pursuit, leaped aboard the timber wagon. He was a backwoods boy himself; he knew how to handle mules. He gave a shout to which the team responded instantly. They leaped ahead just as Ruth came to the side of the long reach that connected the small pair of front wheels with the huge wheels in the rear.

"Get off of that wagon, Fred! " she had just cried, when the mules started. She was directly in front of the large rear wheel. If it struck her—knocked her down—ran over her! Fred knew that she would be killed and he seized her hands and dragged her up beside him on the jouncing timber-reach.

"Now see what you've done! " he bawled, as the mules broke into a gallop.

But Ruth was too frightened for the moment to speak. Her uncle had a pair of mules, and she knew just how hard they were to manage. And this pair were evidently looking toward supper. They flew up the road, directly away from the railroad, and the wagon jounced about so that she could only hold on with both hands.

"Stop them! Stop them! " she cried.

But that was much easier said than done. The animals had been willing enough to start when given the word by a stranger; but now they did not recognize their master's voice when the boy yelled:

"Yea-a! Yea-a! "

Instead of stopping, the mules went faster and faster. They had their bits 'twixt their teeth and were running away in good earnest.

Almost immediately, when the bumping and jouncing wagon got away from the store and the two or three neighboring houses, they were in the deep woods. There were no farms—no clearings—not even an open patch in the timber. The snow lay deep under the pines and firs. The road had been used considerably since the last snow, and the ruts were deep. Therefore the mules kept to the beaten track.

"Oh, stop them! stop them! " moaned Ruth, clinging to the swaying, jouncing cart.

"I can't! I can't! " repeated the terrified boy.

"Oh, you wicked, wicked boy! you'll kill us both! " cried Ruth.

"It's your own fault you're here, " returned Fred, sharply. "And I wouldn't never have got onto the wagon if you hadn't chased me. "

"I believe you are the very worst boy who ever lived! " declared the girl from the Red Mill, in both anger and despair. "And I wish I had let you go your own wicked way. "

"I wish you had, " growled Hatfield, and then tried to soothe the running mules again.

He was successful in the end. He had driven mules before and understood them. The beasts, after traveling at least two miles, began to slow down. The wagon was now passing through a wild piece of the forest, and it was growing dark very fast. Only the snow on the ground made it possible for the boy and girl to see objects at a distance.

Ruth was wondering what her friends would think when they missed her, and likewise how she would ever get back to the railroad. Would Mr. Cameron send back for her? What would happen to her, here in the deep woods, even when the mules stopped so that she dared leap down from the cart?

And just then—before these questions became very pertinent in her mind—she was startled by a wild scream from the bush patch beside the road. Fred cried out in new alarm, and the mules stopped dead—for a moment. They were trembling and tossing their heads wildly. The awful, blood-chilling scream was repeated, and there was the soft thudding of cushioned paws in the bushes. Some beast had leaped down from a tree-branch to the hard snow.

"A cat-o'-mountain! " yelled Fred Hatfield, and as he shouted, the lithe cat sprang over the brush heap and landed in the road, right beside the timber cart.

Once Ruth had been into the menagerie of a traveling circus that had come to Darrowtown while her father was still alive. She had seen there a panther, and the wicked, graceful, writhing body of the beast had frightened her more than the bulk of the elephant or the roaring of the lion. This great cat, crouching close to the snow, its tail sweeping from side to side, all its muscles knotted for another spring, struck Ruth dumb and helpless.

Fortunately her gloved hands were locked about the timber on which she lay, for the next instant a third savage scream parted the bewhiskered lips of the catamount and on the heels of the cry the mules started at full gallop. The panther sprang into the air like a rubber ball. Had the mules not started the beast must have landed fairly upon the boy and the girl clinging to the reach of the timber wagon.

But providentially Ruth Fielding and her companion escaped this immediate catastrophe. The savage beast landed upon the wagon, however—far out upon the end of the timber, beyond the rear wheels. Mad with fright, the mules tore on along the wood road. There were many turns in it, and the deep ruts shook them about terrifically. Ruth and Fred barely retained their positions on the cart—nor was the catamount in better situation. It hung on with all its claws, yowling like the great Tom-cat it was.

On and on plunged the poor mules, sweating and fearful. Ruth and Fred Hatfield clung like mussels to a rock, while the panther bounded into the air, screeching and spitting, always catching the tail of the cart as it came down—afraid to leap off and likewise afraid to hang on.

The mules came to a hill. They were badly winded by now and their pace grew slower. The panther scratched along the reach nearer to the two human passengers, and Ruth saw its eyes blazing like huge carbuncles in the dusk. There was a fork of the roads at the foot of the hill. Fred Hatfield uttered a shriek of despair as the mules took the right hand road and struck into the bush itself—a narrow and treacherous track where the limbs of the trees threatened to brush all three passengers from the cart at any instant.

"Oh! oh! we're done for now! " yelled Fred. "They've taken the road to Rattlesnake Hill. We'll be killed as sure as fate! "

CHAPTER VIII

FIRST AT SNOW CAMP

Fred Hatfield's fears might have been well-founded had the mules not been so winded. They had run at least four miles from the railroad and even with the fear of the snarling panther behind them they could not continue much farther at this pace.

But over this rougher and narrower road the timber cart jounced more than ever. In all its life the panther had probably never received such a shaking-up. The mules had not gone far on what Fred called the Rattlesnake Hill Road when, with an ear-splitting cry, the huge cat leaped out from the flying wagon and landed in the bush.

"We're saved! " gasped Ruth. "That dreadful beast is gone. "

Fred immediately tried to soothe the mules into a more leisurely pace; but nothing but fatigue would bring them down. Thoroughly frightened, they kept starting and running without cause, and there was no chance in this narrow road to turn them.

The fact that it ascended the side of the hill steeply did more toward abating the pace of the runaways than aught else. The track crept along the edge of several abrupt precipices, too—not more than thirty or forty feet high, but enough to wreck the wagon and kill mules and passengers had they gone over the brink.

These dangerous places in the winding road were what had so frightened young Hatfield at first. He knew this locality well. But to Ruth the place was doubly terrifying, for she was lost—completely lost.

"Oh, where are we going? What will become of us? " she murmured, still obliged to cling with both hands to the jumping, rocking reach.

The mules could gallop no longer. Fred yelled at them "Yea-a! Yea-a! " at the top of his voice. They began to pay some attention—or else were so winded that they would have halted of their own volition. And as the cart ceased its thumping and rumbling a light suddenly blazed up before them, shining through the dusk, and higher up the hill.

"What is that? A house? " cried Ruth, seizing Fred by the shoulder.

Not more than half an hour ago the girl from the Red Mill had slipped out of the private car at the Emoryville Crossing, in pursuit of the runaway youth; now they were deep in the wilderness and surrounded by such dangers as Ruth had never dreamed of before.

The baying of a hound and the angry barking of another dog was Ruth's only answer. She turned to see Fred Hatfield sliding down off the cart.

"You sha'n't leave me! " cried Ruth, jumping down after him and seizing the runaway desperately. "You sha'n't abandon me in this forest, away from everybody. You're a cruel, bad boy, Fred Hatfield; but you've just *got* to be decent to me. "

"What did you interfere for, anyway? " he demanded, snarling like a cross dog. "Lemme go! "

But if Ruth was afraid of what terrors the forest might hold, and of her general situation, she had seen enough of this boy to know that he was just a poor, miserable coward—he aroused no fear in her heart.

"I'm going to just stick to you, Freddie, " she assured him. She was quite as strong as he, she knew. "You are going home. At least, you shall go back to Mr. Cameron—"

Just then the flare of light ahead broadened and a gruff voice shouted:

"Hullo! what's wanted? Down, Tiger! Behave, Rose! "

The dogs instantly stopped their clamor. The light came through the open door and the glazed window of a little hut perched on a rock overlooking the road. The mules had halted just below this eminence, and Ruth saw that there was a winding path leading up to the door of the hovel. Down this path came the huge figure of a man, with the two dogs gamboling about him in the snow. The occupant of this cabin in the wilderness carried a rifle in one hand.

"Hullo! " he said again. "That's Sim Rogers's team—I know those mules. Are you there, Sim? What's happened ye? "

"Who is it? " whispered Ruth, again, still clinging to Fred's jacket.

"It's—it's the Rattlesnake Man, " returned the boy, in a shaking voice.

"Who is he? " asked Ruth, in surprise.

"He lives here alone on the hill. He's a hermit. They say he's crazy. And I guess he is, " added Fred, with a shudder.

"Why do you think he's crazy? "

But before Fred could reply—if he intended to—the hermit reached the road. He was an old but very vigorous-looking man, burly and stout, with a great mat of riotous gray hair under his fur cap, and a beard of the same color that reached his breast. He seemed to have very good eyes indeed, for he immediately muttered:

"Ha! Sim's mules—been running like the very kildee! All of a sweat, I vow. Two young folks—ha! Scared. Runaway—ah! What's that? "

The dogs began to bay again. Far behind the boy and girl—down the hill road—rose the eyrie scream of the disappointed panther.

"That cat-o'-mountain chase ye, boy? " the hermit asked, sharply.

But Fred had no answer. He stood, in Ruth's sharp clutch, and hung his head without a word. The girl had to reply:

"I never was so scared. The beast jumped right on the cart and we just shook him off down the hill yonder. "

"A girl, " said the hermit, talking to himself, but talking aloud, in the same fashion as before. Without doubt, being so much alone in these wilds he had contracted the habit of talking to himself—or to his dogs—or to whatever creature chanced to be his company.

"A girl. Not Sim's gal. Sim ain't got nothing but louts of boys. Let me see. What boy is this? "

"He is Fred Hatfield, " said Ruth, simply. Fred jumped and tried to pull away from her; but Ruth's hold was not to be so easily broken. The hermit, however, seemed to have never heard the name before. He only said, idly:

"Fred Hatfield, eh? You his sister? "

"No, sir. I am Ruth Fielding, " she replied.

"Ruth Fielding? Don't know her. She's not belongin' around here. No. Well, how'd you get here? And with Sim's mules? "

Ruth told him briefly, but without bringing Fred Hatfield's trouble into the story. They had got aboard the timber cart at the crossing, the mules had run away, the panther had taken a ride with them and— here they were!

The hermit merely nodded in acknowledgment of the tale. His questions dealt with her alone:

"Where do you belong? "

"The party I was with are bound for Snow Camp. Do you know where that is, sir? " Ruth asked.

"Not ten miles away. Yes. "

"They will be worried—"

"I will get you over there before bedtime. Go up to my house and wait. This boy and I will stable the mules in my barn; it's just along the road here. Sim will follow the beasts and find them; but he'll be some time in getting along. He lives along this road himself —not far, not far. Ah! "

The old man talked mostly as though he spoke to himself. He seldom more than glanced at her, his eye roving everywhere but at the person to whom he spoke. Ruth started toward the house from which the fire and lamplight shone so cordially. The dogs stood before her—Tiger, the big hound, and Rose, a beautiful Gordon setter,

"Let her alone, " said the hermit to his canine companions. "She's all right. "

The dogs seemed to agree with him immediately. The hound sniffed once at the hem of Ruth's frock; Rose gambolled about her and licked her hand. Ruth now realized how cold she was, and she ran quickly up to the open door of the cabin.

On the threshold she hesitated a moment. A great lamp with a tin shade, hanging from the rafters, illuminated all the center of the room. At one end burned a hot log fire on the hearth; but the two further corners were in gloom. Ruth had said she had never seen a log cabin, and it was true. This one seemed to her to be a very cozy place indeed, even if it was the habitation of a hermit.

As she entered, however, she found that there was a rather suffocating, unpleasant odor in the place. It was light, yet penetrating enough to be distinguished clearly. In one of the darker corners was what appeared to be a big green chest, and it had a glazed window frame for a cover. Something rustled there.

The dogs followed her in and she sat down in an old-fashioned, bent hickory chair on the hearth—perhaps the hermit himself had just risen from it, for there was a sheepskin lying before it for a mat and a pair of huge carpet slippers on either side of the sheepskin. The dogs came in and sat down by the slippers, just where Ruth could rest a hand on either head, and so blinked at the flames while they waited for the return of the hermit and the runaway boy.

So she sat when they came into the cabin, stamping the snow from their shoes. The hermit led Fred by the arm. He had not overlooked the care with which Ruth had retained him by her side.

"So you want to go over to Mr. Parrish's Snow Camp? " asked the old man.

"It belongs to Mr. Cameron, now. " said Ruth. "I know that there is a telephone there, and I can get word to Mr. Cameron and Helen and Tom at Scarboro that we are safe. "

"I'm not going, " said Fred "I'll stay here. "

"You'll go along with Young Miss, " said the hermit, firmly. "I'll git ye a pannikin of tea and a bite. Then we'll start. We'll go 'cross the woods on snowshoes—'twill be easier. "

"Oh, can I do it, do you suppose? " cried Ruth. "I never wore such things in my life. "

"You'll learn, " said the hermit.

He bustled about, making the tea and warming a big pancake of cornbread which he put into an iron dripping-pan down before the glowing coals at one side. While they waited for the water to bubble for the tea the old man went to the big chest, and began to talk and fondle something. Ruth heard the rustling again and turned around to look.

"Want to see my children, Young Miss? " asked the old man, whose eyes seemed as sharp as needles.

Ruth arose in curiosity and approached. Within a yard of the old man and his chest she stopped suddenly with a gasp. The hermit stood up with two snakes twining about his hands and wrists. The serpents ran their tongues out like lightning, and their beady eyes glowed as though living fire dwelt in their heads. Ruth was frightened, but she would not scream. The hermit handled the snakes as though they were as harmless as kittens—as probably they were, the poison sacks having been removed.

"They won't hurt you—harmless, harmless, " said the old man, caressingly. "There, there, my pretties! Go to bed again. "

He lifted the glass cover of the chest and dropped them into its interior. There was a great hissing and rustling. The hermit stepped to the hanging lamp and turned the shade so as to send the radiance of it into that corner. Through the pane Ruth saw a squirming mass of scaly bodies, mixed up with an old quilt. More than one tail, with rows of "buttons" and rattles on it, was elevated, and one angry serpent "sprung his rattle" sharply.

"Hush, hush, my dears! " said the hermit, soothingly. "Go to sleep again now. My children, " he said, nodding at Ruth. "Pretty dears! "

To tell the truth, the girl from the Red Mill wanted to scream; but she held herself down, clenching her hands, and saying nothing. The kettle began to sing and she was glad to go back to the chair by the fire and afterward to sip the tin cup of hot tea that their host gave her, and eat with gocd appetite a square of the crisp cornbread.

Meanwhile, the hermit took from the walls three pairs of great, awkward-looking snowshoes and tightened the lacings and fitted thongs to them. The pair he selected for Ruth looked to the girl to be so big that she never could take a step in them; but he seemed to expect her to try.

They went out of the cabin as the moon was rising. It came up as red and fiery as the sun had gone down. Long shadows of the tall trees were flung across the snow. The hermit commanded Rose, the setter, to guard the hut, while he allowed the hound to follow at heel. He carried his rifle, and Ruth was glad of this.

"Haven't heard a cat-o'-mountain around here this winter, " he said, as they started up the hill. "Didn't hear nor see one at all last winter. Neighbors will have to get up a hunt for this one that troubled you, Young Miss, 'fore it does more damage. "

At the top of the ascent they stopped and the old man put on Ruth's snowshoes for her. Fred, always without a word and looking mighty sullen (but evidently afraid of the rattlesnake man) tied his own in place and the hermit slipped into his and they each gave Ruth a hand.

She stood up and found that her weight made little or no impression upon the well-packed snow. There was no wind and, although the air was very keen (the thermometer probably being almost to the zero mark) it was easy for her to move over the drifts. With some little instruction from the rattlesnake man, and after several tumbles— which were of little moment because he and Fred held her up—Ruth was able to put one foot before the other and shuffle over the snow at a fairly good pace.

The moonlight made the unbroken track as plain as noonday. To Ruth it seemed almost impossible that the hermit could find his way through a forest which showed no mark of any former traveler; but he went on as though it was a turnpike.

Two hours and a half were they on the way, and Ruth had begun to be both tired and cold when they crossed a road on which there were telegraph, or telephone poles and then—a little farther into the Big Woods—they struck a well-defined private track over which sleds had recently traveled.

"You say some of your party and the baggage were coming over to-night, " said the hermit to Ruth. "They have been along. This is the road to Snow Camp—and there is the light from the windows! "

Ruth saw several points of light directly ahead. They quickly reached a good-sized clearing, in the middle of which stood a two-story log cabin, with a balcony built all around it at the height of the second floor. Sleigh bells jingled as the horses stamped in the yard. The heavy sledges with the luggage and the serving people had just arrived. Ruth Fielding was the first of the pleasure party to arrive at Snow Camp.

CHAPTER IX

"LONG JERRY" TODD

Some dogs began barking, and the hermit's hound replied by baying with his nose in the air—a sound to make anybody shiver! The Rattlesnake Man gave a lusty shout, and a door opened, flooding the porch of the big log cabin with lamplight.

"Hello! " came the answering shout across the clearing, and a very tall man—as thin as a lath—strode down from the porch and approached them, after sending back the dogs—all but one. This big creature could not be stayed in his impetuous rush over the snow and the next instant he sprang up and put both his forepaws on Ruth's shoulders.

"Oh, Reno! " she cried, fondling Tom Cameron's big mastiff, that had come all the way from Cheslow with them in the baggage car. "*You* know me; don't you? "

"Guess that proves her right to be here, " said the hermit, more to himself than to the surprised tall man, who was the guide and keeper in charge of Snow Camp. "Your boss lose one of his party off the train, Long Jerry Todd? "

"So I hear. Is this here the gal? " cried the other, in immense surprise. "I swanny! "

"Yep. She's all right. I'll go back, " said the rattlesnake man, without further ado, turning in his tracks.

"Oh, sir! " cried Ruth. "I'm so much obliged to you. "

But the hermit slipped away on his snowshoes and in less than a minute was out of sight. Then Ruth looked around suddenly for Fred Hatfield. The runaway had disappeared.

"Where's that boy? " she cried.

"What boy? " returned Long Jerry, curiously. "Didn't see no boy here. "

"Why, the boy that came here with us. He left the train at Emoryville when I did—you must have seen him. "

"I never did, " declared the guide. "He must have slipped away. Maybe he's gone into the house. You'd better come in yourself. The women folks will 'tend to you. Why, Miss, you're dead beat! "

Indeed Ruth was. She could scarcely stumble with the guide's help to the porch. She had kicked off the snowshoes and the hermit had taken them with him. Had it not been for the hermit and Fred Hatfield, Ruth Fielding would never have been able to travel the distance from the hermit's cabin to Snow Camp. And the terrible shaking up she had received on the timber cart made her feel like singing old Aunt Alvirah's tune of "Oh, my back and oh, my bones! "

There were two maids whom Mr. Cameron had brought along and they, with two men, had come over from Scarboro (a ride of eight miles, or so) with the luggage. They welcomed Ruth and set her down before a great fire in the dining room, and one of them removed the girl's shoes so that her feet might be dried and warmed, while the other hurried to make some supper for the wanderer.

But as soon as Ruth got her slippers on, and recovered a little from the exhaustion of her trip, two things troubled her vastly. She inquired for the boy again, and learned that he had not been seen about the camp. When she and the hermit had entered the clearing, Fred had undoubtedly taken the opportunity to slip away.

"And in the night—and it so cold, too, " thought Ruth. "What will Mr. Cameron say? "

That question brought her to the second of her troubles. Her friends would worry about her all night if she did not find some way of allaying their anxiety.

"Oh, Mary! " she said to the maid. "Where's the telephone? Tom said there was telephone connection here. "

"So there is, Miss, " returned the maid. "And somebody had better tell Mrs. Murchiston that you're safe. They're all as worried as they can be about you, for the folks at that store by the railroad—where the train stopped—when *they* was called up as soon as the train reached Scarboro, declared that you had got run away with by a team of mules. "

"Which was most certainly true, " admitted Ruth. "I never had such a dreadful time in all my life. Run away with by mules, and frightened to death by a great big catamount— —"

Mary squealed and covered her ears. "Don't tell me! " she gasped. "Sure, Miss, there do bes bears, an' panthers, an' wild-cats, an'— an' I dunno what-all in these woods. Sure, me and Janey will never go out of this house whilst we stay. 'Tain't civilized hereabout. "

Ruth laughed rather ruefully. "I guess you're right, Mary, " she said. "It doesn't seem to be very civilized here in the backwoods— and such queer people live here, too. But now! let me telephone. "

The maid showed her where it was and Ruth called up Scarboro and got the hotel where the Cameron party was stopping. Almost immediately she heard Mr. Cameron's voice.

"Hullo! Snow Camp? What's wanted? " he asked, in a nervous, jerky way.

"This is me, Mr. Cameron—Ruth, you know. I am all right at Snow Camp. "

"Well! That's fine! Thank goodness you're safe! " ejaculated the merchant, in an entirely different tone. "Why, Ruth, I was just about sending a party out from the store at Emoryville to beat up the woods for you. They say there is a big panther in that district. "

"Oh, I know it. The beast frightened us most to death—"

"Who was with you? " interrupted Mr. Cameron.

"Why, that boy! He jumped off the train and I followed to stop him. Now he's run away again, sir. "

"Oh, the boy calling himself Fred Hatfield? " ejaculated Mr. Cameron. "He's left you? "

"He came here to Snow Camp and then disappeared. I am sorry—"

"You're a good little girl, Ruth. I wanted to bring him up here—and there are people who would be glad to know who he really is."

"But don't you know? Isn't his name Fred Hatfield?" questioned Ruth, in surprise.

"That can't be. Fred Hatfield was shot here in the woods more than a month ago. It was soon after the deer season opened, they tell me, and it is supposed to have been an accident. Young 'Lias Hatfield, half-brother of the real Fred, is in jail here, held for shooting his brother. Who the boy was whom we found and brought from the Red Mill, seems to be a mystery."

"Oh!" cried Ruth, but before she could say more, Mr. Cameron went on:

"We'll all be over in the morning. I hope you have not taken cold, or overtaxed your strength, I must go and tell Helen. She has been frightened half to death about you. Goodnight."

He hung up the receiver, leaving Ruth in rather a disturbed state of mind. The newspaper clipping that had dropped out of the old wallet the strange boy had carried, was the account of the shooting affair. Mention was made in it about the very frequent mistakes made in the hunting season—mistakes which often end in the death of one hunter by the hand of another.

It said that 'Lias Hatfield and his younger brother, Fred, had had a quarrel and then gone hunting, each taking a different direction. The younger boy had ensconced himself just under the brink of a steep bank at the bottom of which was Rolling River, a swift and deep stream. His brother's story was that he had come up facing this place, having started a young buck not half a mile away. He thought he heard the buck stamping, and blowing, and then saw what he thought was the animal behind a fringe of bushes at the top of this steep river bank.

The hunter blazed away, and heard a dreadful scream, a rolling and thrashing in the brush, and a splash in the river. He ran forward and found his brother's old gun and tippet. There was blood on the bushes. The supposition was that Fred Hatfield had been shot and had rolled into the swift-flowing river. 'Lias had given himself up to the authorities and there seemed some doubt in the minds of the people of Scarboro as to whether the shooting had been an accident.

"If there was no body found," thought Ruth, all the time she was eating the supper that Mary brought her, "how do they know Fred Hatfield is really dead? And if he *is* dead, who is the boy who is traveling about the country using Fred Hatfield's name and carrying Mr. Hatfield's old wallet? I guess Fred has run away, instead of being killed, and is staying away because he hates his brother 'Lias, and wishes him to get into trouble about the shooting. If that's so, isn't he just the meanest boy that ever was?"

Long Jerry Todd came in with a huge armful of wood for the fire, and Ruth determined to pump him about the accident. The tall man knew all about it, and was willing enough to talk.

He sat down beside the fire and answered Ruth's questions most cheerfully.

"Ya-as, I knowed old man Hatfield," he said. "He's been dead goin' on ten year. That Fred wasn't good to his mother. His half-brothers— children of Old Man Hatfield's fust wife—is nicer to their marm than Fred was. Oh, ya-as! he was shot by 'Lias, all right. I dunno as 'Lias meant to do it. Hope not. But they found Fred's body in the river t'other day, and so they arrested 'Lias."

But Long Jerry hadn't seen any sign of the boy that had been with Ruth and the hermit when they arrived at Snow Camp. Ruth did not like to discuss the mystery with him any more; for it *was* a mystery now, that was sure. Fred Hatfield's body had been found in the river, yet a boy was traveling about the country bearing Fred Hatfield's name.

The guide finally unfolded himself and rose slowly to his full height, preparatory to going back to the kitchen regions. He was nearly seven feet tall, and painfully thin. He grinned down upon Ruth Fielding as she gazed in wonder at his proportions.

"I'm some long; ain't I, Miss?" he chuckled. "But I warn't no taller than av'rage folks when I was a boy. You hear of some folks gettin' stunted by sickness, or fright, or the like. Wal, I reckon *I* got stretched out longer'n common by fright. Want to hear about it?"

He was so jolly and funny that Ruth was glad to hear him talk and she encouraged him to go on. So Jerry sat down again and began his story.

CHAPTER X

BEARS—AND OTHER THINGS

"Ye see, " drawled Jerry, "my marm was alive in them days—bless her heart! Dad was killed on the boom down Rolling River when I was a little shaver; but marm hung on till I got growed. Ya-as! I mean till I got clean through growin' and that was long after I voted fust time, " and he chuckled and wagged his head.

"Wal, mebbe I was sixteen; mebbe seventeen. Boys up here in the woods have to cut their own vittles pretty airly. I was doin' a man's labor when I was 'leven. Ya-as, Miss! Had to work for me an' marm.

"And marm worked, too. One day I started for Drownville with a big bundle of aperns marm had sewed for Mis' Juneberry that kep' store at Drownville. She got two bits a dozen for makin' them aperns, I remember. Wal, it was a wilder country then than it is now, and I never see a soul, nor heard the sound of an axe in walking four miles. Just at the end o' them four miles, " continued Long Jerry, his eyes twinkling, "there was a turn in the road. I swung around it—I was travelin' at a good clip—and come facin' up an old she b'ar which riz up on her hind laigs an' said: 'How-d'-do, Jerry Todd! ' jest as plain as ever a bear spoke in its e-tar-nal life!

"Why, " said Long Jerry, almost choking with his own laughter, "by the smile on thet thar b'ar's face and the way she spread her arms wide to receive me, it was plain enough how glad she was ter see me. "

"I should think you'd have been scared to death! " gasped Ruth, looking down at him.

"Wal, I calculate I was some narvous. I was more narvous in them days than I be now. Hadn't seen so much of the world. And sure hadn't seen so much o' b'ars, " cackled Jerry. "Not bein' used to b'ar sassiety I natcherly balked when that ol' she b'ar appeared so lovin'. I had pretty nigh walked right into her arms and there wasn't much chance to make any particular preparations. Fact was, I didn't have nothin' with me more dangerous than a broken jack-knife, and I don't know how it might strike you, Miss, but to me that didn't seem to be no implement with which to make a b'ar's acquaintance. "

"I should think not! " giggled Ruth. "What *did* you do? "

"Wal, first of all I give her marm's bundle—ya-as I did! I pitched that there bundle of aperns right at her, and the way she growled an' tore at 'em was a caution, now I tell ye! I seen at once what she'd do to me if she got me, so I left them parts, an' left 'em quick! I started off through the woods, hittin' only the high spots, and fancied I could beat the old gal runnin'. But not on your tin-type! No, sir-ree! The old gal jest give a roar, come down on all four feet, and started after me at a pace that set me a-thinkin' of my sins.

"Jest as sure as you live, if I'd kept on running she'd had me within thirty yards. An' I knew if I climbed a big tree she'd race me to the top of it and get me, too. Ye see, a small-round tree was my only chance. A b'ar climbs by huggin' their paws around the trunk, and it takes one of right smart size to suit them for climbin',

"I see my tree all right, and I went for it. Missus B'ar, she come cavortin' an' growlin' along, and it did seem to me as though she'd have a chunk out o' me afore I could climb out o' reach. It was jest about then, I reckon, " pursued Long Jerry, chuckling again, "when I believe I began to grow tall!

"I stretched my arms up as fur as I could, an' the way I shinnied up that sapling was a caution to cats, now I tell ye! She riz up the minute she got to the tree and tried to scrape me off with both paws. She missed me by half a fraction of an infinitessimal part of an inch —that's a good word, that 'infinitessimal'; ain't it, Miss? I got it off of a college perfesser what come up here, and he said he got it straight-away out of the dictionary. "

"It's a good word, Mr. Todd, " laughed Ruth, highly delighted at the man and his story.

"Wal! " chuckled Jerry, "we'll say she missed me. I was so scar't that I didn't know then whether she had missed me or was chawin' of me. I felt I was pretty numb like below my waist. And how I did stretch up that tree! No wonder I growed tall after that day, " said Jerry, shaking his head. "I stretched ev'ry muscle in my carcass, Miss—I surely did!

"There was that ol she b'ar, on her hind legs and a-roarin' at me like the Mr. Bashan's Bull that they tell about, and scratchin' the bark off'n that tree in great strips. She cleaned the pole, as far up as she could reach, as clean as a bald man's head. She jumped as far as she could, gnashed her teeth, and tried her best to climb that sapling. Every time she made a jump, or howled, I tried to climb higher. An', Miss, that was the time I got stretched out so tall, for sure.

"The bear, with wide-open mouth, kept on a-jumpin' an' ev'ry time she jumped I clumb a little higher, I was so busy lookin' down at her that I never looked up to see how fur I was gettin' toward the top, so, all of a suddent-like, the tree top begun to bend over with me an' sumpin' snapped. 'Twarn't my galluses, neither! " crowed Long Jerry, very much delighted by his own tale. "I knowed that, all right. Sna-a-ap! she went again, and I begun to go down.

"I swanny! but that was a warm time for me, Miss—it sure was. There was that ol' she b'ar with her mouth as wide open as a church door— or, so it looked to Jerry Todd. They say a feller that's drowndin' thinks over all his hull endurin' life when he's goin' down. I believe it. Sure I do. 'Twarn't twenty feet from the top o' that tree to the ground, but I even remembered how I stole my sister Jane's rag baby when I couldn't more'n toddle around marm's shanty—that's right! —an' berried of it in the hog-pen. Every sin that was registered to my account come up before me as plain as the wart on Jim Biggle's nose! "

"Oh, Mr. Todd! " cried Ruth. "Falling right on that awful bear? "

"That's what I was doin', Miss—and it didn't take me long to do it, neither, I reckon. Mebbe the b'ar warn't no more ready to receive me than I was to drap down on her. I heard her give a startled *whuff,* and she come on all four paws. The next thing I done was to land square on her back—I swanny! that was a crack. Purty nigh drove my spine up through the top of my head, it did. And the ol' b'ar must ha' been mighty sorry arterwards that she was right there to receive me. She give a most awful grunt, shook me off onto the ground and kited out o' that as though she'd been sent for in a hurry! I swanny! I never did see a b'ar run so fast, " and Long Jerry burst into an uproarious laugh.

"But that, I reckon, is the time I got so stretched out an' begun to grow so tall, Miss, " he added. "Stretchin' an' strainin' to git away from that ol' she b'ar was what done it. "

Ruth was delighted with the guide; but she was very tired, too, and when the maids came in she was only too glad to fall in with the suggestion of bed. She was put to sleep in a great, plainly furnished room, where there were three other beds—a regular dormitory. It was like one of the Prime sleeping rooms at Briarwood Hall.

And how Ruth did sleep that night after her adventurous day! The sun shone broadly on the clearing about the camp when she first opened her eyes. Mary put her head in at the door and said:

"Your breakfast will be spoilt, Miss Ruth, or I wouldn't disturb you. All the men's ate long ago and Janey's fussin' in the kitchen. Besides, the folks will be over from Scarboro in an hour. Mr. Cameron just telephoned and asked how you were. "

"Oh, I feel fine! " cried the girl from the Red Mill, joyfully.

But when she hopped out of bed she found herself dreadfully stiff and lame; the jouncing she had received while riding with the boy calling himself Fred Hatfield, and the catamount, on the timber cart, and later her first long walk on snow-shoes, had together strained her muscles and lamed her limbs to a degree. Old Aunt Alvirah's oft-repeated phrase fitted her condition, and she grimly repeated it:

"Oh, my back and oh, my bones! "

But the prospect of the other girls, coming—and Tom and his friends, too—and the fun in store for them all at Snow Camp, soon made Ruth Fielding forget small troubles. Besides, the muscles of youth are elastic and the weariness soon went out of her bones. Before the party arrived from Scarboro she had opportunity of going all about the great log lodge, and getting acquainted with all it held and all that surrounded it.

The great hall on the lower floor was arranged so as to have a broad open fireplace at either end. These fires were kept burning day and night and the great heaps of glowing logs made the hall, and most of the upper rooms, very comfortable indeed. The walls of this hall were hung with snowshoes, Canadian toboggans—so light, apparently, that they would not hold one man, let alone four, but very, very strongly built—guns, Indian bows and sheaf of arrows, fish-spears, and a conglomeration of hunting gear for much of which Ruth Fielding did not even know the names, let alone their uses.

Outside the snow had been cleared away immediately around the great log house and a wide path was cut through the drifts down to a small lake, or pond. In coming from Rattlesnake Hill the night before with the old hermit, and the boy who called himself Fred Hatfield, they had come down a long incline in sight of the camp. Now, Ruth saw that a course had been made level upon that hillside, banked up on either side with dykes of snow, and water poured over the whole to make a perfect slide. There was a starting platform at the top and the course was more than half a mile in length, Long Jerry told her.

But when she had seen all these things sleigh bells were heard and Ruth ran out to welcome her friends.

CHAPTER XI

THE FROST GAMES

The big sleigh in which were Helen and the other girls swept into the clearing in advance and Ruth's chum led the chorus addressed vociferously to the girl from Red Mill.

"Oh, Ruthie! "

"The lost is found! "

"And she got here first—wasn't that cute of her? "

"Oh, *do* tell us all about it, Ruth, " cried Lluella Fairfax.

"However could you scare us so, Ruthie? " cried Jennie Stone, the heavyweight. "I was so worried I was actually sick. "

"And that is positively 'no error, '" laughed Belle Tingley. "For once Heavy was so troubled that she couldn't eat. "

Helen was out of the sleigh at once and hugged Ruth hard. "You blessed girl! " she cried. "I was *so* afraid something dreadful had happened to you. "

"And what became of that horrid boy Mr. Cameron tried to take to Scarboro? " demanded Madge Steele.

The boys piled out of their sledge before Ruth could answer these questions, and she was unable to give a very vivid explanation of all that had happened to her since leaving the train, until the whole party was gathered before one of the open fires in the hall, waiting for dinner. Before this hour came, however, and while the rest of the young folks were getting acquainted with the possibilities of Snow Camp, Ruth had a serious talk with Mr. Cameron regarding the mysterious boy who had disappeared on the verge of the Snow Camp reservation.

"I don't know how he escaped us. He sped away through the woods with the old hermit's snowshoes—I am sure of that. And that old

Rattlesnake Man didn't seem to be bothered at all by his loss, " Ruth said.

"Perhaps that hermit knows something about the fellow. We'll look into that, " said the merchant, gravely. "However, Ruth, you did what you thought was right. It was reckless. I cannot commend you for leaving the train, child. Something dreadful might have happened to you. "

"I thought something dreadful *did* happen to me, " said Ruth, with a shudder, "when those mules ran away and that catamount leaped up on the timber cart. "

"I believe you! And your going to the cabin of that rattlesnake catcher. They say he is mad, and he handles the serpents just as though they were white mice. The people hereabout are afraid of him, " said Mr. Cameron, earnestly.

"He was as kind as he could be to me, " said Ruth, shaking her head. "I don't think I should ever be afraid of him. His eyes are kind. But the snakes—oh! they did frighten me dreadfully. "

"From what I hear of this young man, 'Lias Hatfield, who is in jail at Scarboro, he is a decent lad and has worked hard for his stepmother. The half-brother he shot was about the age of this boy we found down home. But *his* body was recovered from the river only the other day when they arrested 'Lias. I shall make it my business to see the Hatfields personally and learn, if possible, how a stranger like that boy who came here with you, Ruth, could have obtained Mr. Hatfield's old wallet. "

"He had some deep interest in the mystery of this shooting, " declared Ruth, and she told the merchant of the newspaper clipping that had dropped out of the old wallet when she had undertaken to dry the boy's clothing at the Red Mill.

Meanwhile, the other young folks were highly delighted over the possibilities for fun at Snow Camp. Tom and his friends did not pay much attention to what was inside the great log house; but before noon they knew all that was to be done outside and were unhappy only because they did not know which to do first. In addition, Busy Izzy had exhausted himself and every man about the place, asking questions; and finally Tom and Bob gagged him with his own handkerchief and threatened to tie him up and not give him any dinner if he did not stop it.

"But *do* let him ask for a second helping to pudding, boys, " urged the kind-hearted Heavy. "It's going to be fine—I had a taste of the dough. Mary says it's 'Whangdoodle Pudding, with Lallygag Sauce'; but you needn't be afraid of the fancy name she gives it, " added the plump girl, rolling her eyes. "It's just scrumptious! "

They laughed at Heavy's ecstasies, yet all did full justice to the pudding. Such a hearty appetite as everybody had! The snapping cold and the odor of balsam and pine gave a tang to the taste that none of them had ever known before. The girls were full of plans for quiet hours around the great open fires, as well as for the out-of-door fun; but Tom was leader on this first day of the vacation at Snow Camp, and he declared for skating in the afternoon.

Even Mrs. Murchiston went down to the pond.

The boys took turns in pushing her about in an ice-chair. But Mr. Cameron put on skates and proved himself master of them, too. Long Jerry came down to watch them and grinned broadly at the boys' antics on the ice. Jerry was no skater; but he was stringing snowshoes and by the morning would have enough ready for the whole party and promised to teach the young folk the art of walking on them in half a day.

That afternoon on the ice only put an edge on the appetite of the whole party for the frost games. "Plenty of time to make those pine-needle pillows for the girls at Briarwood, if we have a stormy day, " quoth Helen Cameron. "We mustn't mope before the fire this evening. The moon is coming up—big as a bushel and red as fire! Oh, we'll have some fun this night. "

"What now? " demanded Madge Steele. "I see the boys have stolen out after supper. A sleigh ride? "

"No; although that would be fun, " said Helen.

"Oh, dear! Can't we take it easy this evening? " whined Heavy, after a mighty yawn. "I *was* so hungry—"

"You shouldn't give way to that dreadful appetite of yours, Jennie Stone! " cried Belle Tingley. "If there's any fun afoot I want to be in it. "

"Come on! All ready! " shouted the boys outside the house, and the sextette of girls ran to get on their wraps.

They bundled out of the house to find Tom, Bob and Isadore each drawing a long, flat, narrow toboggan. Helen clapped her hands and shouted:

"Fine! fine! See these sleds, girls. "

"We're going to shoot the chutes, Heavy, " sang out Madge. "Do you think you can stand it? "

"Now, don't any of you back out, " Tom said. "Each of us will take two girls on his sled. There's plenty of room. "

"You'd better draw matches for us, " said the irrepressible Heavy. "That is, if you intend drawing *us*—two to each toboggan—to the top of that slide. I never did care much for boys—they are greedy; but which one of you could drag Madge and me, for instance, up that hill? "

"We draw the line at that, " cried Tom. "Those who can't toddle along to the top of the chute needn't expect to ride to the bottom. "

They all hurried off, laughing and shouting. It was a most beautiful moonlight night. Save their own voices, only the distant barking of a fox broke the great silence that wrapped the snow-clad country about. None of the grown folk followed them. The party had the hill to themselves.

It being a race to the hill-top, with the first two girls to take their places on the toboggan of the first boy, naturally Heavy was out of the running, and bound to be last. She came panting to the starting platform, and found Ruth waiting to share Isadore's sled with her.

Tom, with Madge and Belle, had already shot down the icy chute. Bob Steele, with Lluella and Helen before him, dropped over the verge of the platform and their toboggan began to whiz down the pathway, as Jennie plumped down upon the remaining toboggan.

"Come on, Ruthie! You're a good little thing to wait for me—and I guess Tom Cameron didn't like it much, either? He wanted you. "

"Nonsense, Jennie, " returned Ruth, with a laugh. "What does it matter? As long as we all get a slide—"

"Hurry up, now, " cried Busy Izzy, troubled because he was behind his comrades, if the girls were not. "Sit tight. "

He pushed the toboggan over the edge of the drop almost before Ruth was settled behind Jennie. He flung himself upon the sled, sitting sideways, and "kicked" them over the drop. The toboggan struck the icy course and began to descend it like an arrow shot from a bow. Jennie Stone shrieked a single, gasping:

"Oh! "

The toboggan whizzed down the path, with the low, icy dykes on either hand, and so rapidly that their eyes watered and they could not see. It seemed only a breath when the third toboggan shot onto the level at the bottom, and they passed the crew of the first sled already coming back. It was exhilarating sport—it was delightful. Yet every time they started Ruth felt as though the breath left her lungs and that she couldn't catch it again until they slowed down at the bottom of the hill.

She would have felt safer with one of the other boys, too. Isadore Phelps was none too careful, and once the toboggan ran up one of the side dykes and almost spilled them on the course.

"Do look out what you are about, Isadore, " Ruth begged, when they reached the bottom of the slide that time. "If we should have a spill— —"

"Great would be the fall thereof! " grinned Isadore, looking at Heavy, puffing up the hill beside them.

"You take care now, and don't spatter me all over the slide, " said the cheerful stout girl, whose doll-like face was almost always wreathed in smiles.

But Isadore was really becoming reckless. To tell the truth, Bob and Tom were laughing at him. He had been the last to get away each time from the starting platform, and he could not catch up with the others. Perhaps that was the stout girl's fault; but Ruth would climb the hill no faster than Jennie, and so the third toboggan continued far behind the others. As they panted up the hill Tom and his two companions shot past and waved their hands at them; then followed Bob Steele's crew and Helen shouted some laughing gibe at them. Isadore's face grew black.

"I declare! I wish you girls would stir yourselves. Hurry up! " he growled quite ungallantly.

"What's the hurry? " panted Heavy.

"There's nobody paying us for this; is there? Let 'em catch up with us and then we will be—all—to—geth—er—Woof! My goodness me, I'm winded, " and she had to stop on the hill and breathe.

"Go on and leave us. Take one trip by yourself, Isadore, " said Ruth.

"No, I won't, " returned Phelps, ungratefully. "Then they'll all gab about it. Come along; will you? "

"Don't you mind him, Jennie, " whispered Ruth. "I don't think he's very nice. "

They got aboard the toboggan once more and Isadore recklessly flung himself on it, too, and pushed off. At the moment there came a shrill hail from below. Tom was sending up some word of warning—at the very top of his voice.

But the three just starting down the slide could not distinguish his words.

Jennie shut her eyes tight the moment the toboggan lurched forward, so she could not possibly see anything that lay before them. Ruth peered over the stout girl's shoulder, the wind half blinding her eyes with tears. But the moonlight lay so brilliantly upon the track that it was revealed like midday. Something lay prone and black upon the icy surface of the slide.

CHAPTER XII

PERIL—AND A TAFFY PULL

It seemed to Ruth Fielding, as the toboggan dashed down the chute toward that strange object in their course, as though her lips were glued together. She could not speak—she could not utter a sound.

And yet this inaction—this dumbness—lasted but a very few seconds. The thing upon the slide lay more than half way down the hill—a quarter of a mile ahead when her stinging eyes first saw it.

Toward it the sled rushed, gathering speed every moment, and the object on the track grew in her eyes apace. When her lips parted she screamed so that Isadore heard her words distinctly:

"Stop, Izzy! There's something ahead! Look! "

Of course it was foolish to beg of the boy to stop. Nothing could halt them once they had started upon the icy incline. But her cry warned Isadore of the peril ahead.

He echoed her cry, and was as panic-stricken as the girl herself. At first, the thing looked like somebody lying across the slide. Had one of their friends fallen off either of the other toboggans, and been too hurt to rise? Then, the next instant, both Isadore and Ruth knew that the thing was too small for that.

It was really a jacket that Bob Steele had tied about his neck by the arms. On the way down the sleeves had become untied and the jacket had spread itself out upon the slide to its full breadth.

It didn't seem as though such a thing could do the coming toboggan any harm; but Ruth and Isadore Phelps knew well that if it went upon the outspread coat there would be a spill. It would act like a brake to the sled, and that frail vehicle on which the three young folk rode would stop so abruptly that they would be flung off upon the icy course.

Ruth at least understood this peril only too well; but she made no further outcry. Jennie Stone's eyes were still tight shut.

One moment the outspread jacket lay far before them, across the path. The next instant—or so it seemed—they were right upon it.

"Hang on! " yelled Isadore, and shot his boot-heel into the icy surface of the slide.

The toboggan swerved. Jennie uttered a cry. The sled went up the left hand dyke like a bolting horse climbing a roadside wall or a side hill.

In Ruth's ears rang the shouts of their friends, who were coming hastily up the hillside. They could do nothing to help the endangered crew, nor could the latter help themselves.

Up the toboggan shot into the air. It leaped the shoulder of the dyke and—crew and all—darted out into space.

That was certainly an awful moment for Ruth Fielding and her two companions. Jennie's intermittent squeal turned into a sudden shriek— as keen and nerve-racking as the whistle of a locomotive. Isadore Phelps "blew up" with a muffled roar as he turned half a somersault in the air and landed headfirst in a huge snowdrift.

That is how the girls landed, too. At least, if they didn't dive headfirst into the drift, they were pretty well swallowed up in it. And it was providential that they all did find such a soft cushion when they landed.

Their individual shrieks were broken off suddenly by the smothering snow. Their friends, on the other side of the slide, came plunging across the course, and Bob Steele, slipping on the smooth surface, kicked up both feet high in the air, landed with a crash on the small of his back, and finished the slide to the very bottom of the chute in that most undignified position.

Bob's accident turned the whole affair into a most ludicrous scene. Tom Cameron laughed so hard that he scarcely had the strength to help the girls out of the snowdrift. As for Isadore, he had to scramble out by himself—and the soft snow had got down his neck, and he had lost his hat, his ears were full of snow, and altogether he was in what Madge Steele called "a state of mind. "

"Huh! " Izzy growled, "you all can laugh. Wait! I'll get square with you girls, now, you better believe that. "

And he actually started off for the camp in a most abused state. The others could not help their laughter—the more so that what seemed for a few seconds to promise disaster had turned out to be nothing but a most amusing catastrophe.

This ended the coasting for this particular evening, however. Jennie Stone was pried out of the snowdrift last of all, and they all went to the bottom of the hill where Bob Steele sat with his back against a tree trunk, waiting, as he said, for the "world to stop turning around so fast. " His swift descent had made him dizzy.

They all ran back to Snow Camp, catching up with Isadore before he got there with his grouch, and Tom and Bob fell upon the grouch and dumped it into another snowbank—boy and all—and managed in the scuffle to bring Busy Izzy into a better state of mind.

"Just the same, " he declared, "I'll get square with those girls for laughing at me—you see if I don't! "

"A lot of good that'll do you, " returned Tom Cameron. "And why shouldn't they laugh? Do you suppose that the sight of you on your head in a snowbank with your legs waving in the wind was something to make them *weep*? Huh! "

But when they got inside the big hall, where the two fires burned, Izzy forgot his grouch. There was a basket of popcorn and several "poppers" and the crowd of young folk were soon shelling corn and popping it, turning the fluffy, snow-white kernels into big bowls, over which thick cream was poured, and, as Jennie declared, "they ate till they couldn't eat another crumb! "

"Isn't it just grand? " cried Belle Tingley, when the girls had retired to the big room in which Ruth Fielding had slept alone the night before. "I never did know you could have so much fun in the woods in the dead of winter. Helen! your father is just the dearest man to bring us up here! We'll none of us forget this vacation. "

But in the morning there were new things to go and learn. The resources of Snow Camp seemed unending. As soon as breakfast was over there was Long Jerry ready with snowshoes for all. Tom and Helen, as well as Bob Steele, were somewhat familiar with these implements. And Ruth had had one unforgettable experience with them.

But at first there were a good many tumbles, and none of the party went far from the big lodge on this occasion. They came into the mid-day dinner pretty well tired, but oh, how hungry!

"I declare, eating never seemed so good before, " Bob Steele murmured. "I really wish I could eat more; but room I have not! "

Heavy went to sleep before the fire directly after the meal, but was awakened when the girls all trooped out to the kitchen to make molasses taffy. The boys had gone with Long Jerry to try to shoot squirrels; but they came back without having any luck before the girls were fairly in possession of Janey's kitchen.

"Let us help—aw, do! " cried Tom, smelling the molasses boiling on the range and leading the way into the kitchen.

"You can't cook anything good to eat when there are boys within a mile, and they not know it, " sighed Jennie Stone.

"Or be able to keep them out of it, " declared Madge Steele. "I suppose we shall have to let them hang around, Helen. "

"I tell you! " cried Helen, who never would go back upon her twin, and who liked to have him around, "we'll make some nut candy. There's nuts—half a bushel of them. The boys must crack and pick the nuts and we'll make some walnut taffy—it will be lots nicer than plain taffy. "

"Oh, well, that *does* put another face upon the matter, " laughed Lluella Fairfax.

"But they must all three whistle while they're picking out the nuts, " cried Heavy. "I know them! The nut meats will never go into the taffy pan if they don't whistle. "

Tom and his chums agreed to this and in a few minutes they were all three sitting gravely on the big settee by the fire, a flatiron in each boy's lap, each with a hammer and the basket of nuts in reach, and all dolefully whistling—with as much discord as possible. The whistling did certainly try the girls' nerves; but the boys were not to be trusted under any other conditions.

Busy Izzy, however—that arch schemer—had not forgiven the girls for laughing at his overset on the toboggan slide the night before. And as he sat whistling "Good Night, Ladies" in a dreadful minor, he evolved such a plan for reprisal in his fertile mind that his eyes began to snap and he could hardly whistle for the grin that wreathed his lips.

"Keep at it, Mr. Isadore Phelps! " cried Ruth, first to detect Izzy's defection. "We're watching you. "

"Come! aren't we going to have a chance to eat a single kernel? " Izzy growled.

"Not one, " said Helen, stoutly. "After you have the nuts cracked and picked out, we'll spread the kernels in the dripping pans, the taffy will then be ready, we'll pour it over, and then set the candy out to cool in the snow. After that we'll give you some—if you're good. "

"Huh! " grunted Isadore. "I guess I know a trick worth two of that. We'll get our share, fellows, " and he winked at Tom and Bob.

CHAPTER XIII

SHELLS AND KERNELS

The three boys stuck to their work, with only a whisper or two, until there was a great bowl of nutmeats, and Ruth pronounced the quantity sufficient. Meanwhile, the taffy was boiling in the big kettle, and Ruth and Jennie had buttered three dripping pans. They spread the nutmeats evenly in the pans and then set the pans carefully on a snowdrift outside the back door to get thoroughly cold before the taffy was poured thinly over the nuts.

Everybody was on the *qui vive* about the candy then. The girls couldn't drive the boys out of the room. The bubbling molasses filled the great kitchen with a rich odor. Jennie began popping corn with which to make cornballs of the taffy that could not be run into the three pans of nuts.

Isadore Phelps disappeared for possibly three minutes—no longer; and the girls never missed him.

At last the candy could be "spun" and Ruth pronounced it ready to pour into the pans outside. Isadora said he would help—the kettle was too heavy for the girls to carry. He was adjured to be very, very careful and the girls followed him to the door in a body when he carried out the steaming couldron.

"Do pour it carefully, Izzy! " cried Helen.

"If that boy spoils it, I'll never forgive him, " sighed Heavy.

Ruth ran out after him. But Isadore took great care in pouring the mixture into the pans as he had been instructed, and even she had no complaint to make. He hurried back to the kitchen, too, poured the residue of the boiled molasses upon the popcorn and they made up the cornballs at once.

"Come on, now, " said Izzy, in a great hurry. "Give us fellows our share of the cornballs and we'll beat it. We're going skating. We'll help you eat your old candy when we come back.

"Maybe it will be all gone by that time, " said Heavy, slily.

"I wish you joy of it, then, Miss Smartie, " returned Isadore, chuckling. "Come on, fellows. "

They seized their skates and ran away. Isadore could hardly talk for laughter; and he carried a good sized paper bag besides his share of the popcorn balls.

The girls "cleaned up"—for that had been the agreement with Janey when she let them have her kitchen—and then sat down before the hall fire to make pine pillows, of which they were determined to take a number to Briarwood to give to their friends. Helen had bought a lot of denim covers stamped and lettered with mottoes, including the ever-favorite "I Pine for Thee and Likewise Balsam. "

But although they were very merry around the fire, Heavy could not long be content. The popcorn balls disappeared like magic and the stout girl kept worrying the others with questions about the taffy.

"Don't you suppose that candy's cool? I declare! those boys might play a joke on us—they might creep back and steal all three pans. "

"Dear me, Jennie! " cried Ruth Fielding. "If you are so anxious, why don't you run and bring a pan in? We'll see if it's brittle enough to break up. "

Heavy sighed, but put down her work and arose. "It's always I who has to do the work, " she complained.

"Bring the pan in here and break the candy, " advised Madge Steele. "We'll have to watch you. "

Heavy came back with one of the candy pans in short order, bringing a hammer, too, with which to crack the brittle taffy.

"Come! we'll see how it tastes; and if it's good enough, " she added, smiling broadly, "we won't let the boys have even a little bit. They were mean enough to go off skating without us. "

She cracked up a part of the candy, passed the pan around quickly, and popped a piece into her own mouth. In a moment she spat the candy into the fire, with a shriek, and put her hand to her jaw.

"Oh! oh! oh! " she cried.

"What's the matter with you, Heavy? " demanded Helen, startled.

"Oh, I've broken a tooth I believe. Oh! "

"Why were you so greedy? " began Madge, sedately. And then, suddenly, she stopped chewing the bit of candy she had taken into her mouth, and a sudden flush overspread her face.

"Why, here's a piece of nutshell! " cried Lluella.

"How careless those boys were! " Helen added. "They got some of the shells in with the meat. "

"We should have expected it, " Belle cried. "They never should have been trusted to crack the nuts. "

"Oh, girls! " gasped Ruth, who had quickly examined the candy in the pan.

Her voice was tragic, and the others looked at her (all but Madge) in surprise. "What have those horrid boys done? " demanded Jennie Stone.

"They've spoiled it all! " Ruth cried. "There's nothing but shells in the candy. They've ruined it! "

"Oh! oh! oh! " shrieked Heavy again. "It can't be true! "

"It can be, for it is! " said Madge Steele, decidedly. "Those mean boys! I certainly will fix Bob for that. "

"And Tom! " cried Helen, almost in tears. "How could he be so mean? "

"I don't believe Tom did it, Helen, " said Ruth, slowly.

"He was just as bad as the others, I venture to say, " Madge said, sharply.

"If he is, I won't speak to him for a month! " cried his twin sister. "We won't have anything more to do with them while we are here—there now! Oh, how mean! "

"Maybe it's only one pan that is this way, " suggested Heavy, timidly.

They all ran out to see. The other pans were just like the first one. The nut meats had been removed and shells scattered in the pans instead. No wonder Isadore Phelps had wanted to pour the molasses taffy!

"And they've got all the meats, " said Belle Tingley. "They are eating them and chuckling over the trick right now, I wager. "

"It's a mean, mean trick! " gasped Helen, in a temper. "I never will forgive Tom. And I just hate those other boys. "

"You're welcome to hate Bobbie, " said Madge. "He deserves it. "

"*Such* a contemptible joke! " groaned Belle.

"Let's make some more, " Ruth suggested. "And we won't give them any. "

"No. I don't want to go all through it again, " Helen said, shaking her head.

At that moment the telephone rang. Ruth was nearest and she jumped up and answered the call. At the other end of the wire an excited female voice demanded:

"Is this Snow Camp? "

"Yes, " replied Ruth, "it is. "

"Mr. Cameron's camp? "

"Yes. But he is not in the house just now. "

"Aren't any of your men-folks there? " queried the excited voice.

"I guess most of the men are drawing in logs for the fires, " said Ruth. "What is the matter? "

"I want to warn you all to look out for the panther. It is supposed to be coming your way—towards Snow Camp. The beast has just killed a pig for us, and was frightened away. It's done other damage to-day among the neighbors' cattle. Do you hear me? "

"Oh, I hear you! " cried Ruth, and then held her hand over the mouthpiece and spoke to the other girls: "That panther—that catamount! " she cried. "It is supposed to be coming this way. Where is your father, Helen? And Long Jerry Todd? "

CHAPTER XIV

A TELEPHONE CHASE

The excited screaming of the other girls brought Mrs. Murchiston to the hall in a hurry. When she heard what had caused the excitement she called the maids, intending to send one of them for Mr. Cameron.

But just then the woman—a farmer's wife along the road—began talking to Ruth again, and the maids learned from her answers into the 'phone the cause of the excitement. Go out into the open when the catamount might be within a couple of miles of the lodge? No, indeed!

Mary threw her apron over her head and sank down on the floor, threatening hysterics. Janey was scared both dumb and motionless. These women who had lived all their lives in towns, or near towns, were not fit to cope with the startling incidents of the backwoods.

The woman on the wire explained to Ruth that she was telephoning all along the line toward Scarboro, warning each farmer of the big cat's approach.

"But if it keeps on in the same direction it was going when we saw it last, the creature will strike Snow Camp first, " declared the excited lady. "You must get your men out with guns and dogs to stop the beast if you can. It's mad with hunger and it will do some dreadful damage if it is not killed. "

Ruth repeated this to her friends, and asked Mrs. Murchiston what they should do.

"If the baste comes here, " cried Mary, the maid, "he can jump right into these low winders. We'll be clawed to pieces. "

"There are heavy shutters for these windows, " Mrs. Murchiston said, faintly. "But they are to heavy for us to handle—and I suppose they are stored in one of the outbuildings, anyway. "

"Why, I wouldn't go out of doors for a fortune! " cried Lluella Fairfax.

"But the creature isn't here yet, " Ruth said, doubtfully.

"How do you know how fast he's traveling? " returned Helen, quickly.

"But think of the boys down there skating, " said her chum.

"Oh, oh! " gasped Jennie. "If that panther eats them up they'll be more than well paid for spoiling our taffy. "

"Hush, Jennie! " commanded Madge. "This is no time for joking. How are we going to warn them—and the men in the woods? "

"And father? " cried Helen Cameron.

"Oh, I wouldn't *dare* go out! " gasped Belle Tingley.

But Ruth ran out into the big kitchen and opened the door. The outbuildings were not far away, but not a soul appeared about them. There seemed to be a brooding silence over the whole place. The men were so deep in the woods that she could not hear a sound from them; nor was the ring of skates on the pond apparent to her ear.

"Come back, Ruth! come back! " begged her chum, who had followed her. "Suppose that beast should be hiding near? "

"I don't suppose he's within a mile of the camp, " said Ruth, her voice unshaken. "There are all the guns in the hall—even the little shotguns. I don't suppose the men have a gun with them, and of course the boys have not. And both parties should be warned. I'm going——"

"Oh, Ruth! you're mad! " cried Helen. "You mustn't go. "

"Who'll go, then? " demanded her friend. "I guess we're all equally scared—Mrs. Murchiston and all. "

"Nobody will go——"

"I'm going! " declared Ruth, firmly. "If the panther is coming from that woman's house—the woman who telephoned—then the pond is in the very opposite direction. I'll take Tom's rifle and some cartridges. "

"But you don't know how to shoot! " cried Helen.

"We ought to know. It's a shame that girls don't learn to handle guns just like boys. I'm going to get Long Jerry Todd to show me how. "

While she spoke she had run into the hall and caught up Tom's light rifle. She knew where his ammunition was, too. And she secured half a dozen cartridges and put them into the magazine, having seen Tom load the gun the day before.

"You'll shoot yourself! " murmured Helen.

"I hope not, " returned Ruth, shaking her head. "But I hope I won't have a chance to shoot the panther. I don't want to see that awful beast again. "

"I don't see how you dare, Ruth Fielding! " cried Helen.

"Huh! It isn't because I'm not afraid, " admitted her chum. "But somebody must tell those boys, dear. "

Ruth had already seized her coat and cap. She shrugged herself into the former, pulled the other down upon her ears, and catching up the loaded gun ran out of the kitchen just before Mrs. Murchiston, who had suddenly suspected what she was about, came to forbid the venture. Ruth, however, was out of the house and winging her way down the cleared path toward the pond, before the governess could call to her.

"Oh, she will be killed, Mrs. Murchiston! " cried Helen, in tears.

"Not likely, " declared that lady. "But she should not have gone out without my permission. "

Nor was Ruth altogether as courageous as she appeared. She did not suppose that the huge cat that had so frightened her and the strange boy that Mr. Cameron had brought up from Cheslow, was very near Snow Camp as yet. Yet she glanced aside as she ran with expectation in her eyes, and when of a sudden something jumped in the bushes, she almost shrieked and ran the faster.

There was a crash beside the path, the bushes parted, and a great, fawn-colored body leaped out into the path.

"Oh, Reno! " Ruth cried. "I never *was* so frightened! You bad dog—I thought you were the cat-o'-mountain. "

But immediately she felt that her fear was gone. Here was Tom's faithful mastiff, whose tried courage she knew, and which she knew would not fail her if they came face to face with the panther.

She hurried on, nevertheless, to the pond, to warn the boys; but to her surprise, as she approached the ice, she heard nothing of the truants. There was no ring of steel on the ice, nor were their voices audible. When Ruth Fielding reached the ice, the pond was deserted.

"Now what could have happened to them? Where have they gone? " thought the girl.

She hesitated, not alone staring about the open pond, but looking sharply on either side into the snow-mantled woods. Reno remained by her and she had a hand upon his collar. Should she shout? Should she call for Tom Cameron and his mates? If she called, and the terrible cat was within earshot, it might be attracted to her by the sound.

"Baby! " she finally apostrophized herself. "I don't suppose that beast is anywhere near. Here goes! " and she raised her clear voice in a lusty shout.

There came, however, no reply. She shouted again and again, with a like result.

"Where under the sun could those boys have gone? " was her unspoken question. "Could they have returned to the house by some other path? "

But she did not believe this was so. Rather, she was inclined to think Tom and his comrades had gone farther than the pond. There was a good-sized stream through which the waters of this pond emptied into Rolling River. That outlet was frozen over, too, and it would be just like the three boys to explore the frozen stream.

Ruth wished that she had brought her skates instead of the gun with her. She felt now that the boys should indeed be warned of the roaming panther, as they had gone so far from the lodge. Here was Reno, too. If she told the mastiff to find Tom, he would doubtless do so. She could even send some written word to the boys by the dog—had she a pencil and paper. It would not be the first time that Reno had played message-bearer.

But the warn Tom and his companions would not be all Ruth had started out to do. Tom was a good shot and a steady hand, she knew. With this loaded rifle in his hand the party might feel fit to meet the panther, if it so fell out. Without any weapon even the noble mastiff might prove an insufficient protection.

CHAPTER XV

THE BATTLE IN THE SNOW

It was a fact that Ruth was tempted to run back to the house, just as fast as she could go, and from there send Reno out to find his young master. Whether the dog could have traced Tom on the ice, however, is a question, for Ruth did not yield to this cowardly suggestion. She had come out with the gun to find the boys, and her hesitation at the edge of the pond was only momentary.

She started down the pond toward the stream, seeing the scratches of the boys' skates leading in that direction. There could be no doubt as to where they had gone. Ruth only wished that she had brought her skates when she ran so hastily from Snow Camp.

Not a sound reached her ears, save the sharp twitter of a sparrow now and then, the patter of Reno's feet on the ice, and the rattle of the loaded rifle against the buttons of her sweater-coat. The forest that surrounded the pond seemed uninhabited. The axes of the woodsmen did not echo here, and the boys must indeed be a great way off, for she could distinguish no sound whatever from them.

Yet she had no doubt that she was following their trail—not even when she came down to the outlet of the pond. The strokes of the skates upon the ice were still visible. The three boys had certainly gone down the frozen stream.

"Come on, Reno! " she exclaimed aloud, encouraging herself in her duty. "We'll find them yet. They certainly could not have gone clear to Rolling River—that's ten miles away! "

The stream was not ten yards across—nothing more than a creek. The woods and underbrush shut it in closely. There was not a mark in the snow on either hand of footsteps—not that Ruth could see. And how heavy the afternoon silence was!

Ruth had recovered in a measure from the first fear she had felt of the marauding panther. The beast, had he traveled toward Snow Camp, was likely miles away from the spot. She had determined to go on and find Tom and the others, more that they might be warned of peril on approaching Snow Camp, than for any other reason.

And she did wish, now, that Tom and the other boys would appear. She was more than a mile—quite two miles, indeed—from the lodge.

"I guess Mr. Cameron will call me reckless again. He suggested that I was that when I followed Fred Hatfield—or whatever his name was— from the cars at Emoryville. He'll surely scold me for this, " thought Ruth.

She kept on down the stream, however, and at last began to shout for her boy friends. Her clear voice rang from wall to wall of the forest; but it could not have been heard far into the snowy depths on either hand. Suddenly Reno growled a little, sniffed, and the hair upon his neck began to rise.

"Now, there's no use your doing that, boy, " Ruth declared, clutching the mastiff tight by the collar with her left hand, while she balanced the rifle in her right. "If you hear them, bark! Tom will know it's you, then, and your bark will carry farther than my voice, I do believe. "

Reno whined, and looked from side to side, sniffing the keen, still air. It seemed as though he scented danger, but did not know for sure from which direction it was coming.

"You're scaring me, acting so, Reno! " exclaimed Ruth. "I wish you wouldn't. I can't help feeling that the panther is right behind me somewhere. Oh! "

The end of her soliloquy was a shriek. Something flashed through the brush clump on her left hand. Reno broke into a savage barking and sprang toward the bank. But Ruth did not lose her grip on his collar, and her hand restrained him.

"Oh, Tom! Tom! " the girl cried.

There was another movement in the bushes. It was between Ruth and the way to the camp, had she been so foolish as to try to reach the house directly through the woods. But she did face up stream again, and had Reno been willing to accompany her she would have run as hard as ever she could in that direction.

"Come, Reno! Come, good dog! " she gasped, tugging at his collar. "Let it alone—we must go back— —"

Reno uttered another savage growl and sprang upon the bank. The hard packed snow crunched under him. There sounded a scream from the brush —a sound that Ruth knew well. The catamount was really at hand—there could be no mistaking that awful cry, once having heard it.

The dog burst through the bushes with such a savage clamor that Ruth was indeed terrified. She sprang after him, however, hoping to drag him back from any affray with the panther. What would Tom Cameron say if anything happened to his brave and beautiful Reno?

It was past the girl's power, however, to stay the mastiff. With angry barks he broke through the barrier and entered a small glade not a stone's throw from the bank of the stream. Before Ruth reached this cleared place she saw the tracks of the beast which had so startled her. There could be no mistaking the round impressions of the great, padded paws. Unlike the print of the bear, or the dog, that of the cat shows no marks of claws unless it be springing at its prey.

And now, when Reno burst into the open, the panther uttered another fierce and blood-chilling scream. Ruth noted the flash of the great, lithe body as the beast sprang into the air. Startled for the moment by the on-rush and savage baying of the dog, the panther had leaped into a low-branching cedar. The tree shook to its very tip, and to the ends of its great limbs. There the panther crouched upon a limb, its eyes balefully glaring down upon the leaping, growling mastiff.

As Ruth remembered the creature from the time of her dreadful ride on the timber cart with the so-called Fred Hatfield, it displayed a temper and ferocity that was not to be mistaken. Reno's sudden onslaught was all that had driven it to leap into the tree. But there it crouched, squalling and tearing the hard wood into splinters with its unsheathed claws. In a moment it would leap down upon the dog, and Ruth was horror-stricken.

"Oh, Reno! Good dog! " she moaned. "Come back! come back! "

The mastiff would not obey and in a moment the huge cat sprang out of the tree directly upon Tom Cameron's faithful companion. Reno was too sharp to be easily caught, however; he leaped aside and the sabre-like claws of the panther missed him. Nor was the dog unwise enough to meet the panther face to face.

He sprang in and bit the cat shrewdly, and then got away before the beast wheeled, yelling, to strike him. Round and round in the snow they went, so fast that it was impossible for Ruth to see which was dog and which was cat, their paws throwing up a cloud of snow-dust that almost hid the combatants.

"Ah! " cried Ruth, aloud. "I've missed my chance, I should have tried to shoot the creature while it was in the tree. "

And that seemed true enough. For had she been the best of shots with the rifle, it looked now as though she was as likely to shoot Reno as the panther whilst they battled in the snow.

CHAPTER XVI

AN APPEARANCE AND A DISAPPEARANCE

The dog's snapping barks and the squalling of the catamount stilled every other sound to Ruth Fielding's ears. She had fallen back to the edge of the clearing, and knew not what to do.

She feared desperately for Reno's safety; but for the moment did not know what she might do to help the faithful beast.

She tripped upon a branch and fell to her knees, and the butt of the rifle which she had clung to, struck her sharply in the side.

"Oh! if I had only learned to use a gun! " gasped the distracted girl. "*Could* I shoot straight enough to do any good, if I tried? Or would I kill the poor dog? "

At the moment Reno expressed something beside rage in his yelping. He sprang out of the cloud of snow-spray with an agonized cry, and Ruth saw that there was blood upon his jaws, and a great gash high up on one shoulder.

"Oh! the poor fellow! Poor Reno! " gasped Ruth Fielding. "He will be killed by that hateful brute. "

Spurred by this thought she did not rise from her knee, but threw the barrel of the gun forward. It chanced to rest in the crook of a branch—the very branch over which she had tripped the moment before. She drew the butt of the gun close to her shoulder; she drew back the hammer and tried to sight along the barrel. Suddenly she saw the tawny side of the panther directly before her—seemingly it was at the end of the rifle barrel.

The beast was crouching to leap. Ruth did not know where Reno then was; but she could hear him whimpering. The mastiff had been sorely hurt and the panther was about to finish him.

And with this thought in her mind, Ruth steadied the rifle as best she could and pulled the trigger. The sharp explosion and the shriek of the panther seemed simultaneous. Through the little drift of smoke she saw the creature spring; but it did not spring far. One hind leg hung useless—there was a patch of crimson on the beaten snow—the huge cat, snarling and yowling, was going around and around, snapping at its own leg.

But that flurry was past in a moment. The snow-dust subsided. Ruth had sprung to her feet, dropping the rifle, delighted for the moment that she should have shot the panther.

But she little knew the nature and courage of the beast. On three legs only the huge cat writhed across the clearing, having spied the girl; and now, with a fierce scream of anger, it crouched to spring upon Ruth. She seemed devoted to the panther's revenge, for she was smitten with that terror which shackles voice and limb.

"Oh, Reno! Reno! " she whispered; but the sound did not pass her own lips. The dog was not in sight He lay somewhere in the bushes, licking his wounds. The fierce panther had bested him, and now crouched, ready to spring upon the helpless girl.

With a snarl of pain and rage the beast leaped at her. Its broken leg caused it to fall short by several yards, and the pain of the injured limb, when it landed, caused the catamount to howl again and tear up the snow in its agony.

Ruth could not run; she was rooted to the spot. She had bravely shot at the creature once. Better had it been for her had she not used the rifle at all. She had only turned the wrath of the savage cat from Reno to herself.

And Ruth realized that she was now its helpless quarry. She could neither fight nor run. She sank back into the snow and awaited the next leap of the panther.

At this very moment of despair—when death seemed inevitable—there was a crash in the bushes behind her and a figure broke through and flung itself past her. A high, shrill, excited voice cried:

"Give me that gun! Is it loaded? "

Ruth could not speak, but the questioner saw instantly that there were cartridges in the magazine of Tom Cameron's gun. He leaped upright and faced the crouching cat.

The panther, with a fearful snarl, had to change the direction of its leap. It sprang into the air, all four paws spread and its terrible claws unsheathed. But its breast was displayed, too, to the new victim of its rage.

Bang!

The rifle spat a yard of fire, which almost scorched the creature's breast. The impact of the bullet really drove the cat backward—or else the agony of its death throes turned the heavy body from its victim. It threw a back somersault and landed again in the snow, tearing it up for yards around, the crimson tide from its wounds spattering everything thereabout.

"Oh, it's dead! " cried Ruth, with clasped hands, when suddenly the beast's limbs stiffened. "You've killed it! "

Then she had a chance to look at the person who had saved her.

"Fred Hatfield! " she cried. "Is it you? Or, who *are* you? for they all say Fred Hatfield is dead and buried. "

"It doesn't matter who I am, Ruth Fielding, " said the strange lad, in no pleasant tone.

"Never mind. Come and see Mr. Cameron. Come to the camp. He will help you— —"

"I don't want his help, " replied the boy. "I'll help myself—with *this*, " and he tapped the barrel of the rifle.

"But that belongs to Tom— —"

"He'll have to lend it to me, then, " declared the boy. "I tell you, I am not going to be bound by anybody. I'm free to do as I please. You can go back to that camp. There's nothing to hurt you now. "

At the moment Ruth heard voices shouting from the frozen stream. The boys were skating back toward the pond, and had heard the rifle shots.

"Oh, wait till they come! " Ruth cried.

"No. I'm off—and don't any of you try to stop me, " said the boy, threateningly.

He slipped on the snowshoes which he had kicked off when he sprang for the rifle, and at once started away from the clearing.

"Don't go! " begged Ruth. "Oh, dear! wait! Let me thank you. "

"I don't want your thanks. I hate the whole lot of you! " returned the boy, looking back over his shoulder.

The next moment he had disappeared, and Ruth was left alone. She made a detour of the spot where the dead panther lay and called to Reno. The mastiff dragged himself from under a bush. He was badly cut up, but licked her hand when she knelt beside him.

"Hello! who's shooting over there? " cried Tom Cameron from the stream.

"Oh, Tom! Tom! Come and help me! " replied Ruth, and in half a minute the three boys, having kicked off their skates, were in the glade.

"Merciful goodness! " gasped Bob Steele. "See what a beast that is! "

Tom, with a cry of pain, dashed forward and fell beside Ruth to examine the mastiff.

"My poor dog! " he cried. "Is he badly hurt? What's happened to him? "

"Did she shoot that panther? " demanded Isadore Phelps. "Look at it, Tom! "

"Reno isn't so badly hurt, Tom, " Ruth declared. "I believe he has a broken leg and these cuts. He dashed right in and attacked the panther. What a brave dog he is! "

"But he never killed the beast, " said Bob. "Who did that? "

"Who was shooting here? Where's the gun, Ruth? " Tom demanded, now giving some attention to the dead animal.

Ruth related the affair in a few words, while she helped Tom bind up Reno's wounds. The young master tore up his handkerchiefs to do duty as bandages for the wounded dog.

"We'll carry him to camp—we can do it, easily enough, old man, " said Bob Steele.

"And what about the panther? Don't we want his pelt? " cried Isadore.

"We'll send Long Jerry after that, " Tom said. "I wish that fellow hadn't run away with tiy rifle. But you couldn't help it, Ruth. "

"He certainly is a bad boy, " declared the girl. "Yet—somehow—I am sorry for him. He must be all alone in these woods. Something will happen to him. "

"Never mind. We can forgive him, and hope that he'll pull through all right, after he saved you, Ruthie, " Tom said. "Come on, now, Bobbins. Lend a hand with the poor dog. "

Tom had removed his coat and in that, for a blanket, they carried Reno through the woods to the camp. It was a hard journey, for in places the snow had drifted and was quite soft. But in less than an hour they arrived at the lodge.

The men had come in with the wood by that time, and Mr. Cameron with them. Mrs. Murchiston and the girls were greatly worried over Ruth's absence and the absence, too, of the three boys. But the death of the catamount, and the safety of all, quickly put a better face upon the situation.

Ruth was praised a good bit for her bravery. And Mr. Cameron said:

"There's something in that poor boy whom we tried to return to his friends—if the Hatfields *are* his friends. He does not lack courage, that is sure—courage of a certain kind, anyway. I must see to his business soon. I believe the Hatfields live within twenty miles of this place, and in a day or two I will ride over and see them. "

"Oh! let us all go, father, " urged Helen. "Can't we go in the sleighs we came over in from Scarboro? "

“Don’t take them, sir, ” said Mrs. Murchiston. “I shan’t feel safe for them again until we get out of these woods. ”

“Why, Mis’ Murchiston, ” drawled Long Jerry, who had come into the hall with a great armful of wood, “there ain’t a mite of danger now. That panther’s killed—deader’n last Thanksgivin’s turkey. There may not be another around here for half a score of years. ”

“But they say there are bears in the woods, ” cried the governess.

“Aw, shucks! ” returned the woodsman. “What’s a b’ar? B’ar’s is us’ally as skeery as rabbits, unless they are mighty hungry. And ye don’t often meet a hungry bear this time o’ year. They are mostly housed up for the winter in some warm hole. ”

“But what would these girls do if they met a bear, Mr. Todd? ” asked Mr. Cameron, laughing.

“Why, this here leetle Ruth Fielding gal, *she’d* have pluck enough to shoot him, I reckon, ” chuckled Long Jerry. “And she wouldn’t be the first girl that’s shot a full growed b’ar right in this neighborhood. ”

“I thought you said there wasn’t any around here, Jerry? ” cried Helen.

“This happened some time ago, Miss, ” returned the woodsman. “And it happened right over yon at Bill Bennett’s farm—not four mile from here. Sally Bennett was a plucky one, now I tell ye. And pretty—wal, I was a jedge of female loveliness in them days, ” went on Long Jerry, with a sly grin. “Ye see, I was lookin’ ‘em all over, tryin’ to make up my mind which one of the gals I should pick for my partner through life. And Sally was about the best of the bunch. ”

“Why didn’t you pick her then? ” asked Tom.

“She got in her hand pickin’ first, ” chuckled Jerry. “And she picked a feller from town. Fac’ is, I was so long a-pickin’ that I never got nary wife at all, so have lived all my life an old bachelder. ”

“But let’s hear about Sally and the bear, ” proposed Ruth, eagerly, knowing what a resourceful story-teller Long Jerry was.

"Come Jerry, sit down and let's have it, " agreed Mr. Cameron, and the party of young folk drew up chairs, before the fire. Long Jerry squatted down in his usual manner on the hearth, and the story was begun.

CHAPTER XVII

LONG JERRY'S STORY

"Ol' man Bennett, " began Jerry Todd, "warn't a native of this neck o' woods. He come up from Jarsey, or some such place, and bringed his fam'bly with him, and Sally Bennett. She was his sister, and as he was a pretty upstandin' man, so was she a tall, well-built gal. She sartain made a hit up here around Scarboro and along Rollin' River.

"But she wasn't backwoods bred, and the other girls said she was timid and afraid of her shadder, " chuckled Long Jerry. "She warn't afraid of the boys, and mebbe that's why the other gals said sharp things about her, " pursued the philosophical backwoodsman. "You misses know more about that than I do—sure!

"Howsomever, come the second spring the Bennetts had been up here, Mis' Bennett, old Bill's wife, was called down to see her ma, that was sick, they said, and that left Miss Sally to keep house. Come the first Saturday thereafter and Bennett, *he* had to go to Scarboro to mill.

"You know jest how lonesome it is up here now; 'twas a whole sight wuss in them days. There warn't no telephone, and it was more than 'two hoots and a holler, ' as the feller said, betwixt neighbors.

"But Old Bill's going to mill left only Miss Sally and the three little boys at home. Bennett had cleared a piece around the house, scratched him a few hills of corn betwixt the stumps the year before, and this spring was tryin' to tear out the roots and small stumps with a pair o' steers and a tam-harrer.

"So, from the door of the cabin he'd built, Sally could see the virgin forest all about her, while she was a-movin' about the room getting dinner for the young 'uns. While she was at work the littlest feller, Johnny, who was building a cobhouse on the floor, yelps up like a terrier:

"'Aunt Sally! Aunt Sally! Looker that big dog! "

"Miss Sally, she turns around, an' what does she see but a big brown bear—oh, a whackin' big feller! —with his very nose at the open door. "

"Oh! " squealed Helen.

"How awful! " cried Belle Tingley.

"A mighty onexpected visitor, " chuckled Jerry. "But, if she was scar't, she warn't plumb stunned in her tracks—no, sir! She gave a leap for the door and she swung it shut right against Mr. B'ar's nose. And then she barred it. "

"Brave girl, " said Mrs. Murchiston.

"I reckon so, ma'am, " agreed the guide. "And then she remembered that Tom and Charlie, the other two boys, were gone down the hill to a spring for a bucket of fresh water.

"There were two doors to the cabin, directly opposite each other, and they'd both been open. The spring was reached from the other door and Miss Sally flew to it and saw the boys just comin' up the hill.

"'Run, boys, run! ' she screams. 'Never mind the water! Drop it and run! There's a b'ar in the yard! Run! Run! '

"And them boys *did* run, but they held fast to their bucket and brought most of the water inter the house with 'em. Then Miss Sally barred that door, too, and they all went to the winder and peeped out. There was Mister B'ar snoopin' about the yard, and lookin' almost as big as one of the steers.

"He went a-sniffin' about the yard, smellin' of everything like b'ars do when they're forragin', s'archin' for somethin' ter tempt his appetite. Suddenly he stood stock still, raised his big head, and sniffed the air keen-like. Then he growled and went straight for the pig-pen.

"'Oh, the pigs! the pigs! ' squealed one of the boys. 'The nice pigs! He'll eat 'em all up! '

"And there was a good reason for their takin' on, " said Jerry, "for their next winter's meat was in that pen—a sow and five plump little porkers.

"'Oh, Aunty Sally, ' cries one of the bigger boys, 'What shall we do? What'll father say when he comes back and finds the pigs killed? '

"Ye see, " continued Long Jerry, shaking his head, "it was a tragedy to them. You folks livin' in town don't understand what it means for a farmer to lose his pigs. Old Bennett warn't no hunter, and wild meat ain't like hog-meat, anyway. If the b'ar got those porkers them young 'uns would go mighty hungry the next winter.

"Miss Sally, she knew that, all right, and when the boy says: 'What shall we do? ' she made up her mind pretty quick that she'd got to *try* ter do sumpin'—yes, sir-ree! She run for her brother's rifle that hung over the other door.

"'I'm goin' to try and shoot that b'ar, boys, ' says she, jest as firm as she could speak.

"'Oh, Aunt Sally! you can't, ' says Tom, the oldest.

"'I don't know whether I can or not till I try, ' says she. She felt like Miss Ruthie did—eh? " and the long guide chuckled. "No tellin' whether you kin do a thing, or not, till you have a whack at it.

"'Don't you try it, Aunt Sally, ' says Charlie. 'He might kill you. '

"'I won't give him a chance at me, ' says she. 'Now boys, let me out and mind jest what I say. If anything *does* happen to me, don't you dars't come out, but go in and bar the door again, and stay till your father comes back. Now, promise me! '

"She made 'em promise before she ventured out of the door, and then she left 'em at the open door, jest about breathless with suspense and terror, while Miss Sally sped across the yard toward the pig-pen. Mister Ba'r, he'd torn down some of the pine slabs at one corner and got into the pen. The old sow was singin' out like all Kildee, and the little fellers was a-squealin' to the top o' their bent. The b'ar smacked one o' the juicy little fellers and begun to lunch off'n him jest as Miss Sally come to the other end o' the pen.

"His back was towards her and he didn't notice nothin' but his pork vittles, " pursued Long Jerry. "She crept up beside him, poked the barrel of the Winchester through the bars of the pen, rested it on one bar, and pulled the trigger. The ball went clear through the old feller's head!

"But it takes more'n one lucky shot to kill a full grown brown b'ar, " Jerry said, shaking his head. "He turned like a flash, and with a horrid roar, made at her, dropping the pig. His huge carcass smashing against the pen fence, snapped a white-oak post right off at the ground, and felled two lengths of the fence.

"But Miss Sally didn't give up. She backed away, but she kept shootin' until she had put three more balls into his big carcass. He sprung through the broke-down fence to get at her; but jest as he got outside, the blood spouted out of his mouth, and he fell down, coughing and dying. 'Twas all over in ten seconds, then. "

"My goodness! " gasped Jennie Stone. "How dreadful. "

"But wasn't she a brave girl? " cried Helen.

"Not a bit braver than Ruthie, " said her twin, stoutly.

"I could almost forgive you for spoiling our taffy after that, Master Tom, " declared Helen. "Is that all the story, Mr. Todd? " she added, as the long guide rose up to go.

"Pretty near all, I reckon, Missy, " he returned. "Nobody didn't never say Sally Bennett was afraid, after she'd saved Bill's meat for him. And that ol' b'ar pelt was a coverin' on her bed till she was married, I reckon. But things like that don't happen around here now-a-days. B'ars ain't so common—and mebbe gals ain't so brave, " and he went away, chuckling.

CHAPTER XVIII

"THE AMAZON MARCH"

There had been no open battle between the girls and the boys over the spoiled taffy; but that night, when the six friends from Briarwood Hall retired to their big sleeping room, they seriously discussed what course they should take with the three scamps who had played them so mean a trick; for even Helen admitted that one boy was probably as guilty as another.

"And that Isadore Phelps had the cheek to ask me how I liked the taffy! " exclaimed Heavy. "I could have shaken him! "

"The panther scare spoiled their 'gloat' over us, that's a fact, " said Madge Steele. "But I intimated to that brother of mine that I proposed to see the matter squared up before we left Snow Camp. "

"I'd like to know how we'll get the best of them? " complained Lluella.

"That's so! Mrs. Murchiston won't let us have any freedom, " said Belle. "She's on the watch. "

"I expect she would object if we tried anything very 'brash, '" said Heavy. "We have got to be sly about it. "

"I do not know how much at fault Tom and Mr. Steele are, " said Ruth, quietly. "But so much has happened since they spoiled the candy, that I had all but forgotten the trick. "

"There now! Ruth will forgive, of course, " said Helen, sharply. "But I won't. They ought to be paid back. "

"Wouldn't it be best to just cut them right out of our good times? " suggested Belle.

"But won't that cut us out of their good times? " urged Heavy. "And boys always do think up better fun than girls. "

"I never would admit it! " cried Madge.

"You always have been a regular Tom-boy, Jennie, " said Lluella.

"You ought to be ashamed to say such a thing, Miss Stone, " added Belle.

"Well, don't they? " demanded the unabashed stout girl.

"Then it's because we girls don't put ourselves out to think up new and nice things to do, " proclaimed Madge Steele.

"Perhaps girls are not as naturally inventive as boys, " suggested Ruth, timidly.

"I won't admit it! " cried Madge.

"At least, " said the girl from the Red Mill,

"We don't want to do anything mean to them just because they were mean to us. "

"Why not? " demanded Belle, in wonder.

"That wouldn't be nice—nor any fun, " declared Ruth, firmly. "A joke—yes. "

"Do you call it a joke on us—spoiling our taffy and stealing the nutmeats? " wailed Heavy.

"What else was it? It was a joke to them. There was a sting to it for us. We must pay them back in like manner, but without being mean bout it. "

"Well now! " cried Helen. "I'd like to see you do it, Ruth. "

"Perhaps we can think of a plan, " said Ruth, gaily. "I for one shall not lose any sleep over it. But if you want to pay them off by showing how much we disapprove of their actions, and have nothing to do with their schemes to-morrow, I will agree. "

"We'll begin that way, " said Madge Steele, promptly. "Treat them in a dignified manner and refuse to join in any games with them. That is what we *can* do. "

"Oh, well, " sighed the irrepressible Heavy. "We're bound to have a dreadfully slow day, then. Good-night! "

It began by being a gray day, too. The sun hidden and the wind sighed mournfully in the pines. Long Jerry cocked his head knowingly and said:

"It's borne in on me, youngsters, that you'll see a bit of hard weather before the New Year—that it do. "

"A snowstorm, Jerry? " queried Helen Cameron, clapping her hands. "Oh, goody! "

"Dunno about it's being so everlastin' good, " returned the guide. "You never see a big snow up in these woods; did ye? "

"No, Jerry; but I want to. Don't you Ruth? "

"I love the snow, " admitted Ruth Fielding. "But perhaps a snowstorm in the wilderness is different from a storm in more civilized communities. "

"And you're a good guesser, " grunted Long Jerry. "Anyhow, unless I'm much mistook, you'll have means of knowin' afore long. "

"Then, " said Helen, to Ruth, "we must get the balsam to-day for our pillows. It won't snow yet awhile, will it, Jerry? "

"May not snow at all to-day, " replied the guide. "This weather we've had for some days has been storm-breeding, and it's been long comin'. It won't be soon past, I reckon. "

This conversation occurred right after breakfast. The boys had seen by the way the girls acted that there was "something in the wind. "

The girls ignored Tom, Bob and Isadore as they chatted at the breakfast table, and at once they went about their own small affairs, leaving the boys by themselves.

Tom and his mates discussed some plan for a few minutes and then Tom sang out: "Who'll go sliding? There's a big bob-sled in the barn and we fixed it up yesterday morning. It will hold the whole crowd. How long will it take you girls to get ready? "

Helen turned her back on him. Ruth looked doubtful, and flushed; but Madge Steele exclaimed: "You can go sliding alone, little boy. We certainly sha'n't accompany you. "

"Aw, speak for yourself, Miss, " growled her brother. Then Bob turned deliberately to Helen and asked: "Will you go sliding, Helen? "

"No, sir! " snapped Helen.

"Aw, let 'em alone, Bob, " said Isadore. "Who wants 'em, anyway? "

Jennie Stone would have replied, only Belle and Lluella shook her. It took two girls to shake Heavy satisfactorily. And the entire six ignored the three boys, who went off growling among themselves.

"Just for a little old mess of candy, " snorted Isadore, who was the last to leave the house.

"That's the way to treat them! " declared Madge, tossing her head, when the boys had gone.

"I don't know, " said Ruth slowly. "We might be glad to have them help us get the pine-needles. "

"I believe you are too soft-hearted, Ruth Fielding, " declared Belle Tingley.

"It's because she likes Tom so well, " said Lluella, slily.

"Well, Tom never did so mean a thing before yesterday, " said Tom's sister, sharply.

"Boys are all alike when they get together, " said Heavy. "It spoils 'em awfully to flock in crowds. "

"What does it do to girls? " demanded Ruth, smiling.

"Gives them pluck, " declared Madge Steele. "We've got to keep the boys down—that's the only way to manage them. "

"My, my! " chuckled Jennie Stone, the stout girl. "Madge is going to be a regular suffragette; isn't she? "

"Well, I guess girls can flock by themselves and have just as good times without their brothers, as with them. "

But Ruth and Helen looked more than doubtful at this point. They knew that Tom Cameron, at least, had been a loyal friend and mate on many a day of pleasure. They couldn't bear to hear him abused.

But the girls felt that they really had reason for showing the boys they were offended. Soon after the departure of Tom and his friends the girls started out with bags to gather the balsam for the pillows. On the back porch they sat down to put on the snowshoes which, by this time, they were all able to use with some proficiency. The three boys, snowballing behind the barn, espied them.

"Hullo! " bawled Busy Izzy. "Here come the Amazons. They're going on their own hook now—haven't any use for boys at all. "

He threw a snowball; but Tom tripped him into a bank of snow and spoiled his aim. "None o' that, Izzy! " he commanded.

"Let 'em alone, " growled Bob Steele. "If they want to flock by themselves, who cares? "

"Not I! " declared Izzy. "Look at the Amazon March. My, my! if they should see a squirrel, or a rabbit, they'd come running back in a hurry. They'd think it was another panther. Oh, my! "

But the girls paid no attention to his gibes and shuffled on into the woods. Helen suddenly saw a snow flake upon her jacket sleeve. She called Ruth's attention to it.

"Maybe the snow will come quicker than Long Jerry thought, " declared the girl from the Red Mill. "See! there's another. "

"Oh, pshaw! what's a little snow? " scoffed Belle Tingley.

But the flakes came faster and faster. Great feathery flakes they were at first. The girls went on, laughing and chatting, with never a thought that harm could befall them through the gathering of these fleecy droppings from the lowering clouds.

CHAPTER XIX

BESIEGED BY THE STORM KING

Tom Cameron and his two friends were so busy setting up a target and throwing iced snow-balls at it, that they barely noticed the first big flakes of the storm. But by and by these flakes passed and then a wind of deadly chill swept down upon the camp and with it fine pellets of snow—not larger than pin-points—but which blinded one and hid all objects within ten feet.

"Come on! " roared Bob. "This is no fun. Let's beat it to the house. "

"Oh, it can't last long this way, " said Isadore Phelps. "My goodness! did you ever see it snow harder in your life? "

"That I never did, " admitted Tom. "I wonder if the girls have come back? "

"If they haven't, " said Bob, "they'd better wait where they are until this flurry is over. "

"I hope they have returned, " muttered Tom, as they made their way toward the rear of Snow Camp.

The snow came faster and faster, and thicker and thicker. Bob bumped square into the side of one of the out-sheds, and roared because he found blood flowing from his nose.

"What do you say about this? " he bellowed. "How do we know we're going right? "

"Here! " cried Isadore. "Where are you fellows? I don't want to get lost in the back yard. "

Tom found him (he had already seized the half-blinded Bob by the arm) and the three, arm in arm, made their way cautiously to the kitchen porch. They burst in on Janey and Mary with a whoop.

"Have the girls got back? " cried Tom, eagerly.

"I couldn't tell ye, Master Tom, " said Mary. "But if they haven't come in, by the looks of you boys, they'd better. "

Tom did not stop to remove the snow, but rushed into the great central hall which was used as a general sitting room.

"Where's Helen—and Ruth—and the rest of them? " he demanded.

"Why, Thomas! you're all over snow, " said Mr. Cameron, comfortably reading his paper before the fire, in smoking jacket and slippers.

"Is it snowing? " queried Mrs. Murchiston, from the warmest nook beside the hearth. "Aren't the girls out with you, Tom? "

"What's the matter, my son? " demanded his father, getting up quickly. "What has happened? "

"I don't know that anything has happened, " said Tom, swallowing a big lump in his throat, and trying to speak calmly. "The girls have not been with us. They went into the woods somewhere to get stuff for their pillows. And it is snowing harder than I ever knew it to snow before. "

"Oh, Tom! " gasped the governess.

"Come! we'll go out and see about this at once, " cried his father, and began to get into his out-of-door clothing, including a pair of great boots.

"Is it snowing very hard, Tom? " queried the lady, anxiously. "What makes you look so? "

For Tom was scared—and he showed it. He turned short around without answering Mrs. Murchiston again, and led the way to the kitchen. The other boys had shaken off the snow and were hovering over the range for warmth.

"Found 'em all right; didn't you? " demanded Bob Steele.

"No. They haven't come in, " said Tom, shortly, and immediately Bob began pulling on his coat again.

"Oh, pshaw! " said Isadore. "They'll be all right"

"Where are Jerry and the others? " Mr. Cameron asked the maids.

"Sure, sir, " said Mary, who was peering wonderingly out of the window at the thick cloud of snow sweeping across the pane, "sure, sir, Jerry and the min went down in the swamp to draw up some back-logs. And it's my opinion they'd better be in out of this storm. "

"I agree with you, Mary, " returned Mr. Cameron, grimly, as he opened the door and saw for the first time just what they had to face. "But perhaps they'll pick up the girls on their way home. Trust those woodsmen for finding their way. "

Tom and Bob followed him out of the house. They faced a wall of falling snow so thick that every object beyond arm's length from them was blotted out.

"Merciful heavens! " groaned Mr. Cameron. "Your sister and the girls will never find their way through this smother. "

"Nor the men, either, " said Tom, shortly.

"Oh, I say! " exclaimed Bob, "It can't snow like this for long; can it? "

"We have never seen a right good snowstorm in the woods, " quoth Mr. Cameron. "From what the men tell me, this is likely to continue for hours. I am dreadfully worried about the girls—"

"What's that? " cried Tom, interrupting him.

A muffled shout sounded through the driving snow. In chorus Mr. Cameron and the two boys raised their own voices in an answering shout.

"They're coming! " cried Bob.

"It is Long Jerry Todd and the men—hear the harness rattling? " returned Tom, and he started down the steps in the direction of the stables.

"Wait! we'll keep together, " commanded Mr. Cameron. "I hope they have brought the girls with them. "

"Oh, but the girls didn't go toward the swamp, " returned his son. "They started due north. "

"Shout again! " commanded Mr. Cameron, and the two parties kept shouting back and forth until they met not far beyond the outbuildings belonging to the lodge. The great pair of draught horses were ploughing through the drifts and the three men were whooping loudly beside them.

"Dangerous work this, for you, sir, " cried Long Jerry. "You'd all better remained indoors. It's come a whole lot quicker than I expected. We're in for a teaser, Mr. Cameron. Couldn't scarce make out the path through the woods. "

"Have you seen the girls, Jerry? " cried Tom Cameron.

"Bless us! " gasped the tall guide. "You don't mean that any of them gals is out of bounds? "

"All six of them went into the woods—toward the north—about two hours ago. They went on snowshoes, " said Tom.

The three woodsmen said never a word, but standing there in the driving snow, at the heads of the horses, they looked at each other for some moments.

"Well, " said Jerry, at last, and without commenting further on Tom's statement; "we'd best put up the horses and then see what's to be done. "

"To the north, Tom? " said his father, brokenly. "Are you sure? "

"Yes, sir. I am sure of it. "

"Is there any house in that direction—within reasonable distance, Jerry? " asked the gentleman.

"God bless us, sir! " gasped the guide. "I don't know of one betwixt here and the Canadian line. The wind is coming now from the northwest. If they are trying to get back to the camp they'll be drifted towards the southeast and miss us altogether. "

"Don't say that, Jerry! " gasped Tom. "We *must* find them. Why, if this keeps up for an hour they'll be buried in the drifts. "

"Pray heaven it hold's off soon, " groaned his father.

The men could offer them no comfort. Being old woodsmen themselves, they knew pretty well what the storm foreboded. A veritable blizzard had swept down from the Lakes and the whole country might be shrouded for three or four days. Meanwhile, as long as the snow kept falling, it would be utterly reckless to make search for those lost in the snow.

Jerry and his mates said nothing more at the time, however. They all made their way to the stables, kicked the drift away from the door, and got the horses into their stalls. They all went inside out of the storm and closed the doors against the driving snow. In five minutes, when the animals were made secure and fed, and they tried to open the doors again, the wind had heaped the snow to such a height against them that they could not get out.

Fortunately there was a small door at the other end of the barn, and by this they all got out and made their way speedily across the clearing to the house—Long Jerry leading the way. Tom and Bob realized that they might easily have become lost in that short distance had they been left to their own resources.

Mr. Cameron was very pale and his lips trembled when he stood before the three woodsmen in the lodge kitchen,

"You mean that to try to seek for the girls now is impossible, Jerry? " he asked.

"What do you think about it yourself, sir? " returned the guide. "You have been out in it. "

"I—I don't expect you to attempt what I cannot do myself—"

"If mortal man could live in it, we'd make the attempt without ye, sir, " declared Long Jerry, warmly. "But neither dogs nor men could find their way in this smother It looks like it had set in for a big blizzard. You don't know jest what that means up here in the backwoods. Logging camps will be snowed under and mules, horses and oxen will have to be shot to save them from starvation. The hunting will be mighty poor next fall, for the deer and other varmints will starve to death, too.

"If poor people in the woods don't starve after this storm, it will be lucky. Why, the last big one we had the Octohac Company had a gang of fifty men shoveling out a road for twenty miles so as to get tote teams through with provisions for their camp. And then men had to drag the tote teams instead of horses, the critters were so near starved. Ain't that so, Ben? "

"Surest thing you know, " agreed one of the other hands. "I remember that time well. I was working for the Goodwin & Manse Company. There was nigh a hundred of us on snow-shoes that dragged fodder from the farmers along Rolling River to feed our stock on, and we didn't get out enough logs that winter to pay the company for keeping the camp open. "

"That's the way on it, Mr. Cameron, " said Long Jerry. "We got to sit down and wait for a hold-up. Nothing else to do. You kin try telephoning up and down the line to see if the girls changed their route and got to any house. "

But when Mr. Cameron tried to use the 'phone he found that already there was a break somewhere on the line. He could get no reply.

They were besieged by the Storm King, and he proved to be a most pitiless enemy. The drifting snow rose higher and higher about the lodge every hour. The day dragged on its weary length into night, and still the wind blew and the snow sifted down, until even the top panes of the first floor windows were buried beneath the white mantle.

CHAPTER XX

THE SNOW SHROUD

It was rather difficult to find trees with the new and fragrant leaves started, at this time of year; therefore Ruth and her companions went rather farther from Snow Camp than they had at first intended. But the warning flakes of snow served in no manner to startle them. The snow had been floating down, and whitening their clothing and adorning the trees with a beautiful icing, for more than half an hour, before anybody gave the coming storm a serious thought.

"Perhaps we'd better go back and not get any stuffing for the pillows to-day, Helen, " said Ruth, doubtfully. "See yonder! isn't that more snow coming? "

"Bah! " exclaimed Lluella, interrupting, "What's a little snow? "

"Cautious Ruthie is usually right, " said Madge Steele, frankly. "Let's go back. "

"But we've scarcely got anything in the bags yet! " wailed Jennie Stone. "All this walk on these clumsy old snowshoes for nothing? "

"Well, we'll just go as far as that grove of small trees that we found the other day, and no farther, " said Helen, who naturally— being hostess—had her "say" about it.

As yet there was no real sign of danger. At least, in the woods the girls had no means of apprehending the approach of the shroud of thick snow that was sweeping out of the northwest. They could not see far about them through the aisles of the wood.

Laughing and joking, the jolly party reached the spot of which Helen had spoken. They set to work there in good earnest to fill their bags with the pungent new growth of the trees, whose bending branches were easily within their reach.

"How this soft snow does clog the snow-shoes, " complained Belle Tingley, removing the racquettes to knock them free.

"But the flakes are smaller now, " said Ruth. "See, girls! it's coming faster and finer. I believe we shall have to hurry back, Helen. "

"Ruth is right, " added Madge Steele, who, as the oldest of the party, should have used her authority before this. "Why! it's coming in a perfect sheet. "

"Sheet! " repeated Jennie Stone, with scorn. "Call it rather a blanket. And a thick one. "

"B-r-r-r! How cold it's grown! " cried Lluella.

"The wind is coming with the snow, girls, " shouted Helen. "Come on! let's bustle along home. This place was never meant for us to be bivouacked in. Why! we'll have Long Jerry Todd, and the boys, and the dogs, and all hands out hunting for us. Dear me! how the wind blows! "

"I can't see, girls! " wailed Belle. "Wait for me! Don't be mean! "

"And don't forget Little Eva! " begged Heavy, tramping on behind and carrying one of the bags. "I declare! I can't see Ruth and Helen. "

"Don't get so far ahead, girls! " sang out Madge Steele, warningly. "We'll get separated from you. "

To their surprise Ruth answered from their left hand—and not far away.

"We're not ahead, girls, " said Ruth, quietly. "Only the snow is falling so thickly that you can't see us. Wait! Let us all get together and make a fresh start. It wouldn't do to get separated in such a storm. "

"Oh, this won't last—it can't snow so hard for long! " cried Jennie. "But we can go on, clinging to each other's jacket-tails. "

The six had come together, and Helen laughingly "counted noses. " "Though we mustn't even count 'em *hard,* " she said, briskly rubbing her own, "or we'll break them off. Isn't it cold? "

"It's dreadful! " wailed Lluella. "The wind cuts right through everything I've got on. I shall freeze if we stand here. "

"We won't stand here. We'll hurry on to the camp. "

"Which way, girls? " demanded Heavy. "I confess I have lost all the points of the compass—and I never did know them too well. "

"Oh, I know the way back, " said Helen, stoutly. "Don't you, Ruth? "

"I believe so, " replied the girl from the Red Mill.

But when they started, Ruth was for one direction and Helen for another. The fact that they did not all think alike frightened them, and Madge called another halt.

"This will never do, " she said, earnestly. "Why, we might be lost in such thick snow as this. "

"I can't walk any farther with this bag and on these old snow-shoes! " cried Heavy. "Say! let's get under shelter somewhere and wait for it to hold up—or until they come and dig us out. "

"We're a nice lot of 'babes in the woods', " sniffed Belle.

"I wish we'd let the boys come with us, " said Helen.

"Won't they have the laugh on us? " observed Madge.

"I don't care if they do, " mourned Lluella. "I wish they were here to help us home. "

"Come, come! " said Ruth, cheerfully. "We ought to be able to help ourselves. Here is a big tree with drooping branches. Let's get under it where the snow is not so deep. It may hold up in a little while, and then we can start fresh. Come around here where the wind won't get at us. "

She led the way and the other girls crowded after her. The low-branched tree broke the force of the gale. Ruth lifted the end of one sweeping branch and her friends all crawled beneath the shelter, and as she followed them Heavy squealed:

"Oh, oh, oh! suppose there should be a bear under here? "

"Nonsense! suppose there should be a griffin—or a unicorn. Don't be foolish," snapped Madge.

They at once found the retreat a perfect windbreak, and became comfortable—all hugging together "like a nestful of owlets," Helen said, and all declared themselves as "warm as toast."

But the wind howled mournfully through the wood, and the snow sifted down with a strange, mysterious "hush—hush—hus-s-sh" that made them feel creepy. Although it was not yet midday, the light was very dim under the thick branches of the tree. The snow became banked high behind them, and Ruth, who was in front, had to continually break away the drifting snow with her mittened hands so that they could see out.

And they could see precious little outside of their den. Just the snow drifting down, faster and faster, thicker and thicker, gathering so rapidly that they all were secretly frightened, although at first each girl tried to speak cheerfully of it.

"If we'd only thought to get Janey to put us up a luncheon," sighed Heavy, "I wouldn't have minded staying here all day. It's warm enough, that's sure."

"My feet are cold," complained Lluella. "I don't believe it will remain warm forever."

"And we couldn't make a fire," said Helen.

"I've matches in my pocket," Ruth said quietly. "I've carried them in a bottle ever since we've been in the woods."

"For pity's sake! what for?" demanded Belle.

"Well—Tom told me to. He does. Helen knows," said Ruth, hesitating.

"Goodness me! it's like being cast away on a desert island," cried Heavy. "Carrying matches!"

"Tom *did* tell us to," admitted Helen, laughing. "But I didn't pay much attention to what he said. I know he told us that we could never tell when matches would come in handy in the woods."

"But we'd set the forest afire—and then see what damage would be done! " cried Belle.

"Not necessarily. Especially in this snow, " returned Ruth, calmly. "If we get very cold, and are delayed for long, we can break the dry branches off underneath this tree—and others like it—and get a fire very easily. Tom told us how to do it. "

"So he did! " cried Helen. "I do believe Ruth never forgets anything she is told. And we may be glad of those matches. "

"Goodness me! " whined Lluella. "Don't talk so dreadfully. "

"How do you mean? " queried Helen.

"As though we'd have to stay here under this old tree so long! It's *got* to stop snowing soon. Or else the men will come after us. "

"Why, we all believe that we shall soon get home, " said Madge cheerfully. "But the boys, or the men, either, couldn't find us in this storm. We will have to be patient. "

Patience was hard indeed to cultivate in their present situation. The minutes dragged by with funereal slowness. Lluella began to sob, and the most cheerful of the party could not keep up her spirits indefinitely.

"Oh, but we'll be all right, I am sure! " quoth Madge. "Don't get down-hearted, girls. "

Helen broke down next and declared that she could not remain idle any longer. "We must move out of this, " she said. "We must find our way back. Why, they might come this way hunting for us and never find us—go right by the tree. We ought to get outside and shout, at least. "

"Don't let's leave this warm shelter, " begged Ruth. "It will be really serious if we move farther from the regular camp instead of toward it"

"But we cannot hear any rescue party shouting for us, nor can they hear us under this drift, " insisted Helen.

"Then we'll go out, one at a time, and shout, " declared Ruth. "Let me try. "

She sprang up and pushed her way through the drift at the mouth of their burrow. Not until she was standing outside did she realize the extent of the storm. The snow was swept across the country in a thick and heavy curtain, with a wind driving it, against which she knew she could not stand.

She could not shout into the teeth of the gale, and her cry was driven back into her own ears as weak as the mew of a kitten.

"Ho! " exclaimed Madge Steele. "They couldn't hear that if they were a stone's throw off. Let *me* give a warwhoop. "

"We're all coming out! " cried the dissatisfied Lluella. "Let's all shout. Oh, girls! we've *got* to get back to the camp. We'll die here. "

They scrambled out of the burrow. The wind smote full against them when once they were in the open. When they raised their voices in chorus it seemed as though there was an answering shout from a certain direction.

"Here we are! here we are! Father! Tom! " shrieked Helen, at the top of her voice.

"Don't go! " begged Ruth. "Let us stick by the tree. It will shelter us. Shout again. "

But the majority of the girls were for setting off at once toward the sound they thought they had heard in the midst of the storm. Again and again they shouted. They clung to each other's hands as they ploughed through the drifts (the snowshoes were of no use to them now) but they did not hear the answering cry again.

At last they stopped, all sorely frightened, Lluella in tears. "What will we do now? " gasped Belle.

"We'd better go back to that tree. We were safe there, " muttered Heavy, her teeth chattering.

But they had drifted with the storm, and when they turned to face it they knew at once that never could they make way against the wind and snow.

"Oh, oh, oh! " wailed Helen. "We're lost! we're lost! "

"Hold up! Be brave! " urged her chum. "We must not give up now. Some other tree will give us shelter. Cling together, girls. We *must* get somewhere. "

But where? It was a question none of them could answer. They remained cowering in the driving snow, utterly confused as to direction, and fast becoming buried where they stood.

CHAPTER XXI

ADRIFT IN THE STORM

"We shall freeze to death if we stay here! "

Madge Steele spoke thus, and the situation precluded any doubt as to the truth of the statement. The six girls from Snow Camp were indeed in peril of death—and all were convinced of the fact.

Lluella Fairfax was in tears, and her chum, Belle Tingley, was on the verge of weeping, too. Helen Cameron had hard work to keep back her own sobs; even Jennie Stone, the stout girl, was past turning the matter into a joke. And Madge Steele was unable to suggest a single cheerful portent.

As they clung to each other in the driving snow they seemed, intuitively, to turn to Ruth Fielding. She was the youngest of the six girls; but she was at this moment the more assertive and held herself better under control than her mates.

It had been against her advice that they had left their temporary shelter under the tree. Now they could not beat their way back to it. Indeed, none of them now knew the direction of the burrow that had sheltered them for more than an hour.

What next should they do?

Although unspoken, this was the question that the five silently asked of the girl of the Red Mill. She had displayed her pluck and good sense on more than one occasion, and her friends looked to her for help. Particularly did Helen cling to her in this emergency, and although Ruth was secretly as terrified as any of her mates, she could not give in to the feeling when her chum so depended upon her.

"Why, we're acting just as silly as we can act! " she cried, speaking loud so that they could all hear her. "We mustn't give up hope. The boys, or Mr. Cameron, will find us. It can't keep on snowing forever. "

"But we're freezing to death! " said Belle, and broke out sobbing like her chum.

"Stop, you silly thing! " cried Madge, trying to shake her. But she was really so cold herself that she could not do this. Indeed, the keen wind would soon make movement impossible if they stood still for long.

"Let's keep moving! " shouted Ruth. "Take hold of hands, girls—two by two. Helen and I will go ahead. Now, Belle, you take Lluella. Madge and Heavy in the rear. Forward—march! "

"This is a regular Amazon March; isn't it? " croaked Heavy, from behind.

"But where shall we march to? " Belle queried.

"We'll keep going until we find some shelter. That's the best we can do. Indeed, it is all we *can* do, " replied Ruth.

It was impossible to do more than drift before the gale. Ruth knew this, and likewise she was confident that they were by no means getting nearer to the camp when they followed such a course. But she hoped to find some shelter before the weakest of the girls gave out.

This was Lluella Fairfax. She was delicately built, and unused to muscular exertion of any kind. She seldom took up any gym work at Briarwood, Ruth knew; therefore it was not strange that she should be the first to give out.

For, although the sextette of girls went but a short distance, and traveled very slowly, it was indeed a fearful task for them. The storm drove them on, and suddenly, when Jennie Stone gave utterance to a wild whoop and disappeared from view, Lluella and Belle burst out crying again, and even Madge showed signs of weakening.

"Help! help! " she cried. "She's fallen down a precipice! "

"She's smothered in a snow-bank! " gasped Helen.

Heavy uttered another cry, but seemingly from a great way off. Ruth scrambled back to Madge, and suddenly found her own feet slipping over the brink of some steep descent. She cried out and clung to Madge. Helen took hold of Madge's other hand, and they drew Ruth back to safety.

"Look out! " commanded the older girl. "You'll be down in that hole, too, Ruth. "

"No, no! We must make some attempt to get her up. Jennie! Jennie! where are you? " shrieked Ruth.

"Right under you. Girls! you want to be careful. I've slid down a bank and am standing on what appears to be a narrow shelf along the face of this bank, or hill. And the snow isn't drifted here. Come down. "

"Oh, I wouldn't dare! " cried Lluella.

"If the place will afford us any shelter from this awful wind, why not? " demanded Helen. "We might try it. "

"How deep are you down, Jennie? " asked Madge.

"Only a few feet. You couldn't ever haul me up, anyway, " and the stout girl laughed, hysterically. "You know how heavy I am. "

"Let me try it, " said Ruth, eagerly. "Here's where Jennie slid over. Look out, below! "

"Oh, come on! you can't hurt me, " declared the stout one, and in a moment Ruth had slipped over the edge of the bank and had landed beside Heavy.

"It's all right, girls! " shouted Ruth at once. She could see that the shelf widened a little way beyond, and was overhung by a huge boulder in the bank, making a really admirable shelter—not exactly a cave, but a large-sized cavity.

After some urging, Lluella and Belle allowed themselves to be lowered by Madge and Helen over the brink of the bank. Then Helen herself slid down, and then the oldest girl. When Miss Steele landed upon the shelf beside them, she cried:

"This is just a mercy! Another five minutes up there in the wind and snow, and I don't believe I could have walked at all. My, my! ain't I cold! "

The six girls cowered together under the overhanging rock. The snow blew in a thick cloud over their heads and they heard it sifting down through the trees below them. They were upon a steep side-hill—the wall of a steep gully, perhaps. How deep it was they had no means of knowing; but several good-sized trees sprouted out of the hill near their refuge. They could see the dim forms of these now and then as the snow-cloud changed.

But although they were out of the beat of the storm, they grew no warmer. More than Madge Steele complained of the cold within the next few minutes. Ruth, indeed, felt her extremities growing numb. The terrible, biting frost was gradually overcoming them, now that they were no longer fighting the blast. Exertion had fought this deadly coldness off; but Ruth Fielding knew that their present inaction was beckoning the approach of unconsciousness.

CHAPTER XXII

THE HIDEOUT

Helen had drawn close to her chum and they sat upon the pile of leaves that had blown into this lair under the bank, with their arms about each other's waists.

"What do you suppose will become of us, Ruthie? " Helen whispered.

"Why, how can we tell? Maybe the boys and Long Jerry are searching for us right now——"

"In this dreadful storm? Impossible! " declared Helen.

"Well, that they *will* search for us as soon as it holds up, we can be sure, " Ruth rejoined.

"But, in the meantime? They may be hours finding us. And I am sure I would not know how to start for Snow Camp, if the storm should stop. "

"Quite true, Helen. "

"We won't an-n-ny of us start for Snow Camp again! " quavered Lluella Fairfax. "We'll be frozen dead—that's what'll happen to us. "

"I *am* dreadfully cold, " said Madge. "How are you, Heavy? "

"Stiff as a poker, thank you! " returned the irrepressible. "I haven't any feet at all now. They've frozen and dropped off! "

"Don't talk so terribly! " wailed Belle. "We are freezing to death here. I am sleepy. I've read that when folks get drowsy out in a storm like this they are soon done for. Now, isn't that a fact, Madge Steele? "

"Nonsense! " exclaimed the older girl; but Heavy broke in with:

"It strikes me that now is the time to make use of Ruth's matches. Let's build a rousing fire. "

"How? " demanded Helen. "Where can we get fuel? It's all under the snow. "

"There's plenty of kindling right under *us*" declared Jennie Stone, vigorously. "And Ruth spoke about the under branches of these trees being dry— —"

"And so they are, " declared Ruth, struggling to her feet. "We must do something. A rousing fire against this rock will keep us warm. We can heat the rock and then draw the fire out and get behind it. It will be fine! "

"Oh, I can't move! " wailed Lluella.

"Luella doesn't want to work, " said Madge. "But you get up and do your share, Miss! If you freeze to death here your mother will never forgive me. "

Of course, it would be Heavy that got into trouble. She made a misstep off the platform and sunk to her arm-pits in a soft bank of snow, and it was all the others could do to pull her out. But this warmed them, and actually got them to laughing.

"I believe that laughing warms one as much as anything, " said Madge.

"Ha, ha! " croaked Heavy, grimly. "*Your* laughing hasn't warmed *me* any. I'm wet to my waist, I do believe! "

"We shall have to have a fire now to dry Jennie, " said Ruth. "Now take care. "

They had all abandoned their snowshoes long since, and the racquettes would have been of no use to them in the present emergency, anyway. But Ruth and Madge got to the nearest tree, and fortunately it was half dead. They could break off many of the smaller branches, and soon brought to the platform a great armful of the brush.

Ruth's matches were dry and they heaped up the leaves and rubbish and started a blaze. The other girls brought more fuel and soon a hot fire was leaping against the side of the rock and its circle of warmth cheered them. They got green branches of spruce and pine and brushed away the snow and banked it up in a wall all about the platform, which served them for a camp. Then they scraped the fire out from the rock, threw on more branches (for the green ones would burn now that the fire was so hot) and crowded in between the blaze and the rock.

"This is just scrumptious! " declared Heavy. "We sha'n't freeze now. "

"Not if we can keep the fire going, " said Helen.

Being warm, they all tried to be cheerful thereafter. They told stories, they sang their school songs, and played guessing games.

Meanwhile, the wind shrieked through the forest above their "hideout, " and the snow continued to fall as though it had no intention of ever stopping. The hours dragged by toward dark—and an early dark it would be on this stormy day.

"Oh, if we only had something to eat! " groaned Heavy. "Wish I'd saved my snow-shoes. "

"What for? " demanded Bell. "What possible good could they have been to you, silly? "

"They were strung with deer-hide, and I have heard that when castaway sailors get very, very hungry, they always chew their boots. I can't spare my boots, " quoth Jennie Stone, trying to joke to the bitter end.

The wind wheezed above them, the darkness fell with the snow. Beyond the glow of the pile of coals on the rocky ledge, the curtain of snow looked gray—then drab—then actually black. Moon and stars were far, far away; none of their light percolated through the mass of clouds and falling snow that mantled these big wastes of the backwoods.

"Oh! I never realized anything could be so lonely, " whispered Helen in Ruth's ear.

"And how worried your father and Mrs. Murchiston will be, " returned her chum. "Of course, we shall get out of it all right, Helen; but *did* you ever suppose so much snow could fall at one time? "

“Never! ”

“And no sign of it holding up at all, ” said Madge, who had overheard.

“Sh! Belle and Lluella have curled up here and gone to sleep, ” said Helen.

“Lucky Infants, ” observed Madge.

“I’m going to sleep, too, ” said Heavy, with a yawn.

“There is no danger now. We’re as warm as can be here, ” Ruth said. “Why don’t you take a nap, Helen? Madge and I will keep the first watch—and keep the fire burning. ”

“Suppose there should be wolves—or bears, ” whispered Helen.

“Ridiculous! no self-respecting beast would be out in such a gale. They’d know better, ” declared Madge Steele, briskly.

“And if one does come here, ” muttered Jennie, sleepily, “I shall kill and eat him. ”

She nodded off the next moment and Helen followed her example. Madge and Ruth talked to keep each other awake. Occasionally they fought their way to the half-dead tree and brought back armfuls of its smaller branches.

“It’s a shame, ” declared Miss Steele, “that girls don’t carry knives, and such useful things. Did you ever know a girl to have anything in her pocket that was worth carrying—if she chanced by good luck to have a pocket at all? Now, with a knife, we could get some better wood.”

“I know, ” Ruth admitted. “I know more about camping out than ever I did before. Next time, I’m going to carry things. You never know what is going to happen. ”

As the evening advanced the cold became more biting. They stirred up the fire with a long stick and the glowing coals threw out increased warmth. The four sleeping girls stirred uneasily, and

Madge, putting her hand against the back wall of rock, found that it had cooled.

"When it comes ten o'clock, " she said, consulting the watch she carried, "we'll wake them up, make them stir around a bit, and we'll drag all these coals over against the rock again. Then we'll heap on the rubbish and heat up the stones once more. We ought to keep warm after that till near daylight. "

"The smut is spoiling our clothes, " said Ruth.

"I don't know as that matters much. I'd rather spoil everything I've got on than run the risk of freezing, " declared Madge, with conviction.

They did what they could to keep the other girls warm; but before the hour Madge had proposed to awaken them, Lluella roused and cried a little because she was so chilly.

"My goodness me, Lu! " yawned Heavy, who was awakened, too, "you are just the *leakiest* person that I ever saw! You must have been born crying! "

"I never heard that we came into the world laughing, " said Madge; "so Lluella isn't different from the rest of us on that score. "

"But thank goodness we're not all such snivelers, " grumbled Heavy. "Want me to get up? What for? "

But when Madge and Ruth explained what they intended to do, all the girls willingly bestirred themselves and helped in the moving of the fire and the gathering of more fuel.

"Of course we can't expect any help to-night, " said Helen. "But I know that they'll start out hunting for us at daybreak, no matter whether it keeps on snowing, or not. "

"And a nice time they'll have finding us down in this hole, " complained Belle Tingley.

"Lucky I fell into this hole, just the same, " remarked Heavy. "It just about saved our lives. "

"But I guess we would have been a whole lot better off if we hadn't moved from the first big tree Ruth got us to creep under, " Helen said, thoughtfully. "We couldn't have been more than two miles from Snow Camp then. *Now* we don't know where we are. "

"Never mind that, Helen, " advised Madge. "Help get in the wood. Now, we want a big, rousing fire. We'll just heat that old rock up so that it will stay warm all night. It will be like sleeping as the Russian peasants do—on top of their stoves. "

They had piled the brush on the coals, after scraping the coals back upon the ledge, and the firelight was dancing far up the rock, and shining out into the steadily drifting snow, when suddenly Helen seized her chum's hand and cried:

"Listen! what's that? "

The girls grew silent instantly—and showing no little fear. From somewhere out in the storm a cry came to their ears.

"There it is again, " gasped Helen. "I heard it twice before. "

"I hear it, " repeated Madge. "Wait. "

Again the distant sound came forlornly to their ears. That time they all distinguished it. And they knew that their first hope was quenched. It was no sound of a rescuing party searching for them in the storm, for the word—repeated several times, and unmistakable—they all identified.

"Help! "

CHAPTER XXIII

A DOUBLE CAPTIVITY

"It's a ghost! " gasped Belle as the voice out of the storm died away down the wind.

"So are you! " snapped Madge. "What would a ghost want any help for? Ridiculous! "

"Goodness me! " drawled Heavy. "Seems to me even a disembodied spirit might feel the need of help if it was out in such a gale as this. "

"I mean that we only thought we heard the voice, " chattered Belle.

"Funny we should all think with such unanimity, " scoffed Ruth. "That was certainly a very able-bodied spirit—There! "

Again the cry came brokenly through the storm.

"Somebody lost like ourselves, " said Lluella, with a shiver.

"And he sees the light of our fire, " Jennie Stone urged.

"We must help, whoever it is, " Ruth cried. "Shout, girls! Maybe he wants to know the way—"

"The fire will show him, " said Madge, quickly.

"Perhaps he is hurt! " said Helen.

"Shout! " commanded Ruth.

They raised their voices in a ragged chorus of cries. "Again! " cried Ruth, and that time they sent their halloo out into the storm with more vigor and unanimity. Once more, after they had waited a full minute, they could plainly distinguish the word "Help! "

"This won't do, " said Ruth, briskly. "Whoever it is cannot get to us. "

"And we can't get to him! " cried Lluella.

"I am going to try. I'll go alone. You girls keep hollering. I won't go out of earshot, " promised Ruth.

"Don't do it, Ruthie! You'll be lost, " cried Helen. "Then whatever should we do? "

"I won't get lost—not if you girls continue to shout, " returned her chum.

She had buttoned her coat about her and pulled the skating cap she wore down over her ears, yet not too low to muffle them. Again the cry came wandering through the storm. Ruth started down the bank of the gully; the cry came from the other side of the hollow, she was sure—almost directly opposite the ledge on which they had taken shelter.

When she plunged off the ledge she at once entered the wall of driving, smothering snow. It almost took her breath, it was so deep under her feet and shrouded her about so much like a mantle. Had she ventured this way when first she and her friends had descended to the ledge, Ruth must have actually sunk out of sight in the soft drifts.

But the sifting snow had packed harder and harder as the storm increased. After all, she sank only to her knees and soon found that she was plunging over rather than through the great drifts that filled the gully. How broad this gully was—or how deep when the snow was out of it—she could not imagine. Nor did she give a thought to these things now.

Again she heard the muffled cry for help; but it sounded louder. She had made no mistake in the direction she had taken. The person needing succor was directly in front of the ledge, but could not get over to the fire.

She glanced back over her shoulder. The leaping flames she could not see; but their glow made a round spot of rosy light against the screen of the falling snow. The mystery of the sight terrified her for a moment. Would she ever be able to fight her way back to that ledge?

"Our Father, help me! " was her unspoken prayer, and then she plunged on.

She heard the shrill cries of her friends behind; ahead the lost one shouted out once more.

"Here! here! This way! Help! "

"I'm coming! " responded Ruth Fielding and, beaten as she was by the gale behind, kept steadily on.

The way began to rise before her. She was ascending the other bank of the gully. Suddenly through the snow-wreath that surrounded her she saw something waving. She sprang forward with renewed courage, crying again:

"I'm coming! "

The next moment she seized somebody's gloved hand. "Oh, oh! " cried a shrill, terrified voice. "Who are you? Help me! I am freezing. can't walk—"

"Fred Hatfield! " gasped the amazed girl. "Is it you? What is the matter? "

"Take me to that house. I see the light, but I cannot reach it Help me, for God's sake! " cried the boy.

She could see his white, pinched face as he lay there more than half buried in the snow. His eyes were feverish and wild and he certainly did not know Ruth.

"Help me out! help me out! " he continued to beg. "My leg is caught. "

But it was more weakness and exhaustion than aught else that held the boy in the drift, as Ruth very soon found out when she laid hold of his shoulders and exerted her strength. In a few moments, what with her pulling and his scrambling, the boy was out of the drift.

He had clung to the rifle—Tom Cameron's weapon, of course—and into his belt was stuck a knife and a camp hatchet.

"Why, how did you get here in this storm? " demanded Ruth, as he lay panting at her feet.

"I got lost—from my—my camp, " he responded. "I'm frozen! I can't feel my feet at all—"

"Come across to the fire, " urged Ruth. "We girls are lost from Snow Camp. But we're all right so far. My! how the snow blows. "

Facing the storm they could hardly make headway at all. Indeed, the youth fell within a few yards and Ruth was obliged to drag him through the drifts.

Her friends continued to shout, and occasionally she stood upright, made a megaphone of her hands, and returned their hail. But her strength—all of it—finally had to be given to the boy. She seized him by the shoulders and fairly dragged him toward the other side of the gully, thus walking against the wind, backwards. Occasionally she threw a glance over her shoulder to make sure that she was making straight for the campfire.

The girls' voices drew nearer and finally, at the foot of the slope leading up to the camp, she was forced to halt and drop her burden.

"Come down and help me, Madge! " she cried. "It's a boy—a boy! He can't help himself. Come quick! "

The girls were only a few yards away, but so fiercely did the wind blow that Ruth had to repeat her call for help before Madge Steele understood. Then the big girl dropped down off the ledge and plowed her way toward Ruth and her burden.

"The poor fellow! who is he? " gasped Madge, as together they raised the strange boy and started up the sharp ascent.

"Not Tom! Oh! it's never Tom? " shrieked Helen at the top of the hill.

"No, no! " gasped Ruth. "It's—the—boy—that—ran away. "

They got him upon the dry ledge of rock before the fire. His cheeks showed frostbitten spots, and Jennie began to rub them with snow. "That's the way to treat frostbite, " she declared. "Take off his boots. If his feet *are* frosted we'll have to treat them the same way. "

Helen and Belle obeyed Heavy, who seemed quite practical in this emergency. Ruth had no strength, or breath, for the time being, but lay Reside die fire herself. Meanwhile Madge and Lluella scrapped the red coals out from the rock and swept the platform clean with green branches. Ruth and the runaway boy were drawn into this cozy retreat and soon the boy began to weep and cry out as the heat got into his feet. It was very painful to have the frost drawn out in this manner.

It was now after midnight and the storm still raged. Madge and Jennie floundered out for more fuel. The hatchet the boy carried was of great aid to them in this work and soon they had piled on the ledge sufficient wood to keep the blaze alive until dawn.

By this time the strange youth had been thawed lout and was dropping asleep against the warm rock. Helen and Belle agreed to stand the next watch, and to feed the fire. Both Ruth and Madge needed sleep, the former aching in every muscle from her fight to bring the rescued one in,

"We're doubly captives now, " the girl of the Red Mill whispered to Madge before she dropped asleep. "If it should stop snowing we couldn't try to get back to camp and leave this chap here. And it is certain sure that he could not travel himself, nor could we carry him. "

"You are right, Ruth, " returned Madge. "This addition to our party makes our situation worse instead of better. "

"But maybe it will all come out right in the end, dear. "

"Let us hope so. "

"What a boy of mystery he is! "

"Yes. "

"Do you think we'll ever get to the bottom of his trouble? "

"Let us hope so. "

Then both girls turned over, to get what sleep they could under such trying circumstances.

CHAPTER XXIV

THE SEARCH

It was a most anxious night for everybody at Snow Camp. The thought of the six girls adrift in the blizzard kept most of the household awake, Long Jerry Todd, the guide, remained in the kitchen, on the watch for the first break in the storm. The others retired, all but Mr. Cameron and Tom, who sat before the fire in the living hall.

"I couldn't sleep anyway, " said Tom, "with Helen and Ruth out in the cold. It's dreadful, Dad. I feel that we boys are partly to blame, too. "

"How's that? " his father asked him.

"Why, the girls were mad with us. I let Isadore go too far with his joking, " and he told Mr. Cameron about the spoiled taffy. "If we hadn't done that to them of course they wouldn't have gone into the woods without us—"

"But I am afraid you lads would have been no more cautious than the girls, " interposed Mr. Cameron. "This storm would have taken you by surprise just the same. "

"But we could have been with them and helped them. "

"I have great faith in that little Fielding girl's good sense—and Madge Steele is to be trusted, " said his father. "Don't blame yourself, boy. It was something entirely unforeseen. "

Several times during the night Mr. Cameron tried to communicate with the neighbors over the telephone; but some disaster had overtaken the line and it probably could not be repaired until after the storm.

About five o'clock Long Jerry came into the room. He had been out into the storm, for he was covered with snow.

"How does it look? " asked Mr. Cameron, earnestly.

"She's going to break with sun-up, " prophesied the woodsman. "I've been feeding the cattle and I've got the other men up. If it breaks at all, we three'll start for the neighbors and rouse a gang to help beat the woods. "

"But hadn't we better try to find the girls at once, Jerry? " queried Tom.

"We'll need a large party, Master Tom, " said the guide. "We must cover a deal of ground, and the more men we have who are used to the trail, the better. If it stops snowing we can get around to the neighbors on snowshoes easier than any other way. The drifts are packed hard. I had to tunnel out of the kitchen door. The snow has banked up to the second story gallery. "

"They'll be buried yards under this snow, " groaned Tom.

"Keep up your courage, " said Long Jerry, cheerfully. "If them gals was sharp at all they'd find some shelter and make a fire. "

"If they had matches, " said Mr. Cameron, doubtfully.

"Ruth had matches, I know, " said Tom.

"Oh, we'll find them safe and sound, " declared the guide.

One of Long Jerry's prophecies was fulfilled within the hour. The storm broke. Tom had aroused his friends and the three boys had enlarged the tunnel through the snow from the back porch into the yard, and were shoveling a passageway to the stables. The last flakes of the blizzard fluttered down upon them, and the tail of the gale blew the clouds to tatters and revealed the almost black sky with the stars sparkling like points of living fire.

"Hurrah! " cried Bob Steele. "It's over! "

The guide and the two other men were already getting on their snowshoes, having eaten hurriedly by the kitchen fire. They started out at once to rouse the neighbors. By sunrise the sky was entirely clear and the visitors to the backwoods could climb to the second floor gallery of the lodge and look out over the great drifts. In places the snow was heaped fifteen feet high; but the men shuffled off over these drifts and back again as easily as they would have walked on six inches of snow.

They brought with them six other men, who also sat down to breakfast in the big kitchen, while Mr. Cameron and the boys and Mrs. Murchiston finished their meal in the dining-room. To the surprise of the visitors to the camp, one of the men whom Long Jerry had brought in to help find the girls was the Rattlesnake Man, as he was called.

"We found him poking about the woods by himself, sir, " said Long Jerry, privately, to Mr. Cameron. "He says there's been a boy staying with him for a while back, and that he started out hunting just before the storm. The old hermit was looking for him. By what he says, I believe it's the same boy you folks was bringing up here-the one that claims to be Fred Hatfield. "

"That poor fellow may have lost himself in the blizzard, too, eh? " returned the merchant. "Let us hope we will find them all safely. "

In fifteen minutes the whole party started from the lodge on snowshoes, the boys dragging their toboggans and the men carrying food and hot coffee in vacuum bottles. They separated into four parties; the three boys and Jerry Todd kept together. Jerry believed that the girls would have drifted some with the storm and therefore he struck off due east from the house.

In an hour they came back to the bank of the stream near where Ruth and Reno had their adventure with the panther.

"If old Reno had been well enough to come with us, he would have scented them in a hurry, " declared Tom. "See the creek! it's completely smothered in snow. "

They followed the course of the stream for some distance and found the banks growing more steep. Suddenly Jerry began to sniff the keen air, and in a moment he cried:

"There's a fire near, boys. Somebody is burning pine boughs—and there isn't any house near, that I can swear to! "

They hurried on. Inside of half a mile Isadore descried a column of blue smoke ahead. They began to shout at once, and it was not long before answering cries delighted them.

"That's Madge yelling, " declared Bob. "I'd know her warwhoop anywhere. "

Tom had set out as fast as he could travel, the toboggan jumping after him over the drifts. Even Busy Izzy grew excited, and yelled like a good fellow as he joined in the chase. They all ran down the bed of the stream and reached a deep cut where the banks were very high on either hand.

Up the white slope of the left hand bank was a small plateau on which the fire was burning. Some sort of a camp had been established, surrounded by an embankment of tramped snow. Over this fortress the heads of all six of the girls became visible, all crying out to their rescuers in such a medley of exclamations that no one was understandable.

"Helen! Ruth! " cried Tom. "Are you all right? "

"We're right as right can be, Tommy, " returned his sister, gaily.

"We're not! " squealed Jennie Stone. "We're almost starved to death. If you haven't brought anything for us to eat, don't dare come up here, for we've turned cannibals and we're just about to cast lots to see who should first be sacrificed to the general good! "

But there was more than laughter to season this rescue. Some tears of relief were shed, and even Isadore Phelps showed some shame-faced joy that the catastrophe had resulted in no worse hardships for the girls. He said to Heavy:

"I'm sorry I spoiled that old taffy. If you'd eaten your full share of *that* the other day, I expect you wouldn't have suffered so from hunger. "

The only person who was seriously troubled by the adventure was the strange boy. He had suffered severely In the storm and now he could scarcely move for pains in his back and legs. Otherwise it is doubtful if he would not have run when he heard Long Jerry's voice among the rescuers.

"Great turtle soup! " roared the guide, when he beheld the shrinking, cowering boy. "How did you get here? Do you mean to say you are alive, Fred Hatfield? Why, they buried you—"

"No, they didn't! " snarled the boy. "They only thought they did. "

"And you've let 'em think all this time that you were shot—and poor 'Lias in jail? Well! you always was a mean little scamp, Fred Hatfield! "

But Ruth would not let the guide scold the boy any more. "He's very sick, Mr. Todd, " she said. "He'll have to be carried to the lodge. I believe it is rheumatism, and he ought to have a doctor at once. "

"Lucky he is down and out, then, " muttered the guide, "or I'd be tempted to lay him across my knee and spank him right here and now! "

The girls were very thankful indeed for the hot drink and the food that had been brought. Jerry signaled with his rifle and brought the whole party to the spot within the hour, including the Rattlesnake Man. But when the old hermit saw that the boy was found he would stop no longer.

"Let his folks look after him. I gave him shelter; but he's a bad boy, I reckon. And he doesn't like my children. I don't want anybody about my place that doesn't like my children. Now, that little girl, " he added, pointing to Ruth, "*she* wasn't afraid of them; was you? "

"Not much, " returned Ruth, bravely. "And I'm coming to see you again, sir, if I can. "

"You may come at any time, and welcome, " answered the Rattlesnake Man, with a low bow. "Maybe you would like to learn how to handle my pets, " he added, with a queer grin.

"What, the snakes! " screamed Helen.

"No, I don't think I'd care to do that, " replied Ruth.

"They would not hurt you-they soon learn to know their friends-and they get to be as friendly as kittens, " returned the hermit. "I have a name for each one of them, " he went on, somewhat proudly.

"Maybe I'll-I'll look at them-but I won't want to touch them, " answered Ruth. A few minutes later the strange Rattlesnake Man took his departure.

Fred Hatfield and the girls were all packed upon the sleds and drawn over the snow to the camp, where the rescued and rescuers arrived in safety before noon. But the girls had been through such an experience, and were so exhausted, that as soon as dinner was over they were commanded to go to bed, while one of the men started to town for a doctor to attend young Hatfield.

"And be sure and take this letter to the sheriff, " said Mr. Cameron. "This foolish boy's brother must be released from jail at once. And if his folks want him, they can come here to Snow Camp and take him home, " added the merchant, in some disgust. "I must say that it seems as though pity would be wasted on Fred Hatfield. "

CHAPTER XXV

CERTAIN EXPLANATIONS

But the boy was more seriously ill than any of them suspected at the time. Before night, when the doctor arrived (walking over on snowshoes with the guide) Fred was in a high fever and was rambling in his speech. None of the girls was seriously injured by the adventure in the snow; but the doctor shook his head over Hatfield.

Mrs. Murchiston gave the youth good attention, however, and the doctor promised to come again as soon as a horse could get through the roads. Two days passed before anybody got to Snow Camp saving on snowshoes. The governess was so kind to the sick boy that he broke down and confessed all his wretched story to her.

His home life had not been very happy since his father's death. His brother 'Lias, and the other big boys, were hard-working woodsmen and thought Fred ought to work hard, too, in the woods and on their poor little farm. He had finally had a fierce quarrel with 'Lias and the older boy had thrashed him.

"I only meant to scare him, " Fred confessed, "when he shot at me and thought it was a deer. The bullet whistled right by my head. When I jumped I dislodged a stone in the bank, and that rolled down the hill and splashed into Rolling River. I hid.

"I saw 'Lias was frightened, and I thought it served him right—shooting so carelessly. Lots of folks are shot for deer up here in the hunting reason, and 'Lias is real careless with a gun. So I stayed hid. Then I heard two men talking at night and they said they guessed marm would be glad to get rid of me—I was no good.

"So I got a ride off on the railroad, and I wasn't going back. I didn't know 'Lias had been arrested until Mr. Cameron brought me back up this way and I heard about it from a logger that didn't know me. He said my body had been found. Of course, it wasn't me. Somebody else was drowned in Rolling River. There's been a little French Canadian feller missing since last fall and he was supposed to have been drowned. It was his body they found, I reckon. The man told me the body was so broken and disfigured that nobody could recognize the features—and the clothing was torn all off it.

"I don't know what marm and the boys will do to me if they find me, " wailed Hatfield, who seemed to be more afraid of the rough usage of his big half-brothers than anything else.

But the first sled to get through to Snow Camp brought, besides the doctor, the boy's mother and 'Lias Hatfield himself. The backwoods woman showed considerable tenderness when she met her lost boy, and the young fellow who had suffered in jail for some weeks held no anger against his brother because of it.

"Why, Mr. Cam'ron, " he said to the merchant, "I reckon it sarved me out right. I *was* purty ha'sh with the boy. He ain't naught but a weakling, after all. Marm, she does her best by us all, and we stick to her; but if Fred ain't fitten to work in the woods, or on the farm, we'll find him something to do in town—if he likes it better. I don't hold no grudge. "

Two days later the boy was well enough to move, and they all went away from Snow Camp; but! Mr. Cameron had agreed, before they went, to give Fred Hatfield a chance in his store in the city, if they would send him down there in the spring.

"He's not fit for the rough life up here, " he told Tom and Helen and Ruth, when they talked it over. "He's not an attractive boy, either. But he needs a chance, and I will give him one. If we only helped those people in the world who really *deserved* helping, we wouldn't boost many folks. "

Meanwhile the girls had all recovered from their adventure in the blizzard, and the entire party of young folk found plenty of amusement in the snow-bound camp. In one monstrous heap in the yard the boys excavated a good-sized cavern—big enough so that all the girls as well as the boys could enter it at once; and they lit it up at night with candles and held a "party" there, at which plenty of walnut taffy was served—without shells in it!

"This is heaping coals of fire on your head, young man, " said Madge, tartly, as she passed the pan to Busy Izzy.

"All right, " he returned, with a grin. "Keep on heaping. I can stand it. "

"If you girls had been right smart, " drawled Bob Steele, "when you were lost the other day, you'd have scooped you out a hole like this in a snowbank and hived up as snug as a bug in a rug till the storm was over. "

"Oh, yes! we all know lots of things to do when we are lost again, " returned Helen. "But I hope that our next vacation won't have any such unpleasant experience in store for us. "

"I'm with you in that wish, " cried Belle Tingley.

"Well, now, yo've all promised to go with me to our cottage at Lighthouse Point for two weeks next summer, " cried Heavy. "I guarantee you won't be lost in the snow down there. "

"Not at that time of year, that's sure, " laughed Ruth. "But we don't know yet, Jennie, that we *can* go with you. "

However, it is safe to state here that Ruth, at least, was able to accept the stout girl's invitation, for we shall meet her next in a story entitled: "Ruth Fielding at Lighthouse Point; Or, Nita, the Girl Castaway. "

There was plenty of fun around Snow Camp for the remainder of the ten days they spent there, and when the time came to go back to civilization both girls and boys assured good Mr. Cameron that they had had a most delightful time. They traveled as far as Cheslow together, where Heavy and Belle and Lluella went to their homes for a day or two, to finish out the tag-end of the vacation, while the Steeles and Isadore went home with the Camerons, and Ruth returned to the Red Mill.

And how glad Aunt Alvirah was to see Ruth! Uncle Jabez didn't display his feelings so openly; but Ruth had learned how to take the miller, and how to understand him. She helped him with his accounts, made out his bills for the year, and otherwise made herself of use to him.

"You just wait, Uncle Jabez, " she told him, earnestly. "I'm going to make your investment in my schooling at Briarwood pay you the biggest dividend of anything you ever speculated in—you see. "

"I'm sure I hope so, Niece Ruth, " he grumbled. "I don't much expect it, though. They teach you too many folderols up there. What's *this* now? " he asked, pointing his stubbed forefinger to the little gold and black enamel pin she wore on her blouse.

"'S. B.'"

"Is them the letters? "

"Yes, sir. My society emblem. We're the Sweetbriars, of Briarwood Hall. And you wait! we're going to be the most popular club in the school before long. We've had Mrs. Tellingham, the Preceptress, at one of our meetings. "

"What good is that? " he demanded, shaking his grizzled head.

"Fraternity—fellowship—helpfulness—hope—oh! it stands for lots of things. And then, Uncle Jabez, I am learning to sing and play. Maybe before long I can open the old cottage organ you've got stowed away in the parlor and play for you. "

"That won't lower the price of wheat, or raise the price of flour, " he grumbled.

"How do you know it won't, until we've tried it? " she answered him, gaily.

And so she made the old mill, and the farmhouse adjoining, a much brighter, gayer, pleasanter place while she was in it. Her cheerfulness and sweetness were contagious. Aunt Alvirah complained less frequently of her back and bones when Ruth was about, and in spite of himself, the old miller's step grew lighter.

"Ah, Jabez, " Aunt Alvirah said, as they watched Ruth get into the Cameron automobile to be whisked away to the station, and so to Briarwood for her second half, "that's where our endurin' comfort an' hope is centered for our old age. We've only got Ruthie. "

"She's a mighty expensive piece of property, " snarled the old man.

"Ye don't mean it, Jabez, ye don't mean it, " she returned, softly. "You're thawin' out—and Ruth Fielding is the sun that warms up your cold old heart! "

But this last was said so low that Jabez Potter did not hear it as he stumped away toward the Red Mill.

In the automobile the young folks were having a gay time. Helen was with Ruth, and Tom was on the front seat.

"Say, we sure did have some excitement in Snow Camp as well as fun, " came from Tom.

"And that catamount! " gasped Helen.

"And Ruth's shot! " broke in her twin brother. "Ruth, you ought to try for a marksmanship badge! "

"And wasn't it fine how it came out about Fred, " said Ruth, her face beaming with satisfaction. "I am so glad to know he is no longer a homeless wanderer! "

"All due to you, " said Tom. "Ruth, you're a wonder! " he added, admiringly.

"Oh, Tom! " she answered. Nevertheless, she looked much pleased.

And here let us say good-bye.

THE END

CPSIA information can be obtained at www.ICGtesting.com
Printed in the USA
LVOW040008131211

259072LV00001B/21/A